"That's..." Laurel lost her train of thought.

Xavier's hand settled into the hollow between her neck and shoulder bone and his thumb brushed across her ear.

"Um—we should at least make an appearance. They probably already know we're here."

He didn't release her. "Probably."

"We should go inside."

"We should."

And then he settled his mouth on hers in a long kiss. She dropped into it, greedily sucking up every ounce of sensation as he treated her to his heat and mastery of all things seductive. Their tongues clashed. Awareness and need sizzled along every nerve ending.

He palmed her jaw and angled her head to take her impossibly deeper still, as if he couldn't get enough. Good. She didn't want him to get enough. If he was never sated, he wouldn't stop. That worked for her.

He worked for her. He had something wholly unique that smoldered below the surface, something amazing and intense and profound. It called to her and she couldn't help but answer.

Far too soon, he backed off.

"We should—" He nuzzled her ear and rained little butterfly kisses along her cheek. "Um...go—somewhere."

"Uh-huh." She tilted her head to give his questing mouth better access to lave at her throat. "Like your house?"

* * *

Playing Mr. Right is part of
the Switching Places series from
USA TODAY bestselling author Kat Cantrell!

Dear Reader,

I love stories of people switching places, from *The Prince and the Pauper* to *The Parent Trap*, and I couldn't wait to get to Xavier's story. He's really unhappy with his father for forcing him to switch with his brother, Val. I knew Xavier would have a difficult time being removed from his CEO chair, and an even harder time unbending enough to fall in love. I was right!

Enter Laurel Dixon, a woman whose sole purpose in life is to torture Xavier. Okay, not really, but he sure thinks so! When he hires her to fill an open position at the food bank he's running in Val's stead, it doesn't take long for Laurel to figure out that Xavier's inheritance task needs her hands all over it. He'd rather put his hands on her and have Laurel stay away from his business, but that was never going to happen. Can he get over his resentment of his late father long enough to embrace the partnership Laurel's proposing?

If you missed Val's story, it's available now! Connect with me online at katcantrell.com and let me know which brother you like better. I won't tell. Happy reading!

Kat

KAT CANTRELL

———

PLAYING MR. RIGHT

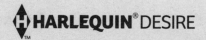
HARLEQUIN® DESIRE

Recycling programs
for this product may
not exist in your area.

ISBN-13: 978-1-335-97176-0

Playing Mr. Right

Printed in U.S.A.

USA TODAY bestselling author **Kat Cantrell** read her first Harlequin novel in third grade and has been scribbling in notebooks since she learned to spell. She's a Harlequin So You Think You Can Write winner and a Romance Writers of America Golden Heart® Award finalist. Kat, her husband and their two boys live in north Texas.

Visit her Author Profile page at Harlequin.com, or katcantrell.com, for more titles.

One

The building housing LeBlanc Charities felt the same as every other time Xavier had set foot in it—like he'd been banished. Despite sharing a last name with the founder, this was the last place he'd choose to be, which was too bad considering he'd been forced to walk through the door nearly every day for the last three months.

And would continue to do so for the next three months until this hell of an inheritance test drew to its conclusion. Xavier's father had devised a diabolical way to ensure his sons danced to his tune long after he'd died: Xavier and his brother, Val, had been required to switch places in order to receive their inheritances.

So the ten years Xavier had spent learning the

ins and outs of LeBlanc Jewelers, plus the five years since he'd taken over the CEO chair and broken his back to please his father…none of that mattered. In order to get the five hundred million dollars he'd have sworn he'd already earned, Xavier had to pass one final test. But instead of being required to do something that made *sense*, the will stipulated that Xavier would become a fundraiser in Val's place at LeBlanc Charities and his brother would assume the reins of LeBlanc Jewelers.

Even three months after the fact, Xavier still foamed at the mouth if he let himself dwell on how unfair and impossible the terms were. His father had betrayed him, bottom line. While Xavier had been putting enormous energy into connecting with his dad and basking in the glow of being the favored son in blissful ignorance, Edward had been plotting to posthumously show his sons how much he really hated both of them.

In that, Xavier and Val were alike. It had been a surprisingly effective bonding experience for the brothers who shared similar faces and not much else. Though twins, they'd never been close, even choosing completely different paths as adults. Val had followed their mother into LeBlanc Charities and thrived. Xavier had gladly shucked off anything remotely resembling charity work in favor of the powerful CEO's office at one of the world's largest and most profitable diamond companies.

All for nothing.

The terms of the will had sliced off a huge piece of Xavier's soul and he'd yet to recover it.

Bitter did not begin to describe his feelings toward his father. But he used that bitterness as fuel. He would not fail at this test. Success was the best revenge, after all.

Xavier had swept into his new role at LBC with gusto…and despite his fierce need to ace his task, he still hadn't gotten his feet under him. It was like his father had stacked the deck against him, somehow. The problem was that the will stipulated Xavier had to raise ten million dollars in donations while doing Val's job. No easy feat. But he hadn't given up yet, nor would he.

Even at 6:00 a.m., LeBlanc Charities teemed with life. The food pantry operated seven days a week, fifteen hours a day. It was ludicrous. A huge waste of capital. Oftentimes, the volunteers reported that no guests had darkened the door of LBC during the early morning hours, yet they always kept the light on.

Changing the operational hours of the food pantry had been one of the first of many executive orders Xavier had come to regret. He'd changed them back, but Marjorie Lewis, the tiny general of a woman who had been a surprisingly effective services manager, had still quit. Sure, she'd told Val—her *real* boss, as she'd informed Xavier—that her mother had fallen ill with a long-term condition. But Xavier knew the truth.

She hated him.

Nearly everyone at LBC did, so that was at least

consistent. The staff who reported to him at LeBlanc Jewelers—his *real* job, as he'd informed Marjorie—respected him. Did they like him? Who knew? And Xavier didn't care as long as they increased profits month over month.

LBC was *not* the diamond industry. No one here *owned* any diamonds, except for him, and he'd stopped wearing his Yacht-Master watch after the first day. Marjorie had pointed out, rather unkindly, that the people LBC helped would either assume it was fake, try to steal it or paint him with the ugly brush of insensitivity. Or all three.

Therefore, a five-hundred-thousand-dollar watch now sat in his jewelry box, unworn. Talk about a waste. But he'd left it there in hopes of garnering some of that mythical respect. Instead, he'd met brick wall after brick wall in the form of Marjorie, who had rallied the troops to hate him as much as she did. And then she'd quit, leaving Xavier holding the bag. Literally.

Yesterday, he'd worked in the food pantry, stocking shopping bags the hungry people LBC served could grab and go. The families took prepacked boxes. Once a day, LBC served a meal, but Xavier stayed out of the kitchen. Jennifer Sanders, the meal services manager, had that well under control and also agreed with the popular opinion that Val walked on water, so anything Xavier did paled in comparison.

Like he did every morning, Xavier retreated to his office. Val's office, really, but Xavier had redecorated. He'd ordered the walls painted and new furniture installed because if this was going to be his domain, it shouldn't remind him every second that Val had been here first—and done it better.

Xavier pushed around the enormous amount of paperwork that a charity generated until his brother popped through the door. Thank God. Xavier had started to wonder if Val would actually show up for their planned meeting about the missing services manager. After Marjorie stormed out, the majority of the day-to-day operations management fell to Xavier and that left precious little time to plan fundraisers that he desperately needed to organize.

Val had offered to help with the interview process, which had been a lifeline Xavier had gladly snagged, without telling his brother how much he needed that help. If the terms of his father's will had taught him anything, it was not to trust a soul, not even family.

"Sorry I'm late." Val strolled into his former office and made a face at the walls, flipping his too-long hair out of his eyes. "If you were going to paint, at least you could have picked a color other than puke green."

"It's sage. Which is soothing."

It was nothing of the sort and did not resemble the color swatch the decorator had showed him in the slightest. But Xavier had to live with it, apparently, because LBC didn't have a lot of extra money for frivolous things like painting. When he'd tried to use his own money, Marjorie had flipped out and cited a hundred and forty-seven reasons that was a bad idea. Mostly what he'd gotten out of her diatribe was that LBC had a negative audit in their rearview and thus had multiple microscopes pointed at their books.

Meaning Xavier needed to watch his step.

"Who do we have on tap today?" Val asked pleasantly as he sprawled in one of the chairs ringing the director's desk that Xavier sat behind.

No one was fooled by the desk. Xavier didn't direct much of anything. He would have claimed to be a smart man prior to this inheritance test, but LBC had slowly stripped away his confidence. At his normal job, he ran a billion-dollar company that was one of the most highly respected jewelry operations in the world. LeBlanc was synonymous with diamonds. He could point to triumph after triumph in his old world. This new one? Still Val's baby even though Xavier's brother was currently helming Le-Blanc Jewelers with flair.

Xavier stopped his internal whining and picked up the single résumé on his desk. "After you ruled out the others, this is the only one. The candidate has experience similar to Marjorie's but with a women's shelter. So probably she's a no-go. I want someone with food-pantry experience."

"Well, that's your call." Val's tone held a tinge of disapproval, as if wanting someone with experience was the height of craziness. "Do you mind if I look at it?"

He handed the résumé to Val, who glanced over it, his lips pursed.

"This Laurel Dixon is the only new résumé you've got?" Val asked.

"From people who are remotely qualified, yeah. So far. I posted the job to the usual sites but we've had very little response."

Val pinched the bridge of his nose. "That's not good. I wonder if our little inheritance experiment has made the rounds. I would have expected more applicants, but if you've scared off all the candidates, I'm going to be in a world of hurt when I step back into my position here."

That stung, but Xavier didn't let it show. He never did. He'd learned to school his emotions at Edward LeBlanc's knee from an early age. CEOs didn't wear their hearts on their sleeves or they lost the respect of their workers. That lesson had served him well—until his father had upended everything in one fell swoop.

"This is not my fault," Xavier responded evenly, though Val's point wasn't lost on him. *Marjorie.* Again. He wouldn't put it past her to have poisoned the well of potential applicants, but there was no way to fix that now. "If you're going to blame anyone, blame Dad."

Val's expression didn't change as he waved the résumé. "We should interview this candidate. What other choice do you have? No one says you have to keep her if she doesn't work out."

"Fine."

Xavier picked up the phone and left a message at the number listed on the résumé. He didn't have time to argue the point or let his feelings get in a twist because Val was throwing his weight around.

This was all temporary, and as Val had so eloquently pointed out, he'd be back in the saddle again soon, anyway. Little that Xavier did would make a difference in the long run.

Since they didn't have much regarding Marjorie's replacement to meet about, after all, Val apparently thought that was a license to ask a few barbed questions about how things were going operationally at LBC. They were interrupted by a brisk knock on the door.

Adelaide, the admin who had been a disciple of Marjorie's, poked her head into the office with a sweet smile for Val. If he hadn't seen it himself, Xavier wouldn't have believed she knew *how* to smile.

"There's a Laurel Dixon here to see you," she said. "About the position."

Xavier had called her less than thirty minutes ago and he'd said nothing about coming by. Only that he'd like to schedule an interview.

"No notice," he said quietly to Val. "That's a little bold, don't you think?"

It tripped his sixth sense and not in a good way. Downtown Chicago was not known for having great traffic patterns, so either she lived really close by or had already been on her way here.

Val raised his brows in challenge. "I'm already impressed. That's the kind of go-getting I like."

Of course he'd say that and manage to make it sound like Xavier was in the wrong at the same time.

"I'd rather send her away and schedule a real interview. After I've had time to go over her qualifications."

"She's here." Val shrugged. "What's there to go over? If you're unsure, I'll do the talking."

"I can talk," Xavier fairly growled. "I just don't like surprises."

Or anyone stepping on his toes, which was what he got for stupidly mentioning to his brother that Marjorie's exodus had caught him sideways. Val had taken full advantage of that show of weakness, too, storming in here like a victorious hero and earning adoring glances from his staff.

Val just grinned and flipped hair out of his face in true slacker fashion. "I'm aware. Don't sweat it. I came by to handle this problem. Let me handle it."

When hell froze over. "We'll both interview her. Adelaide, show her in."

Val didn't even bother to move to another chair like a normal person would. You positioned yourself behind the desk as a show of authority. Val probably didn't even know how to spell authority. That's why his staff loved him, because he treated them all like equals. Except everyone was not equal. Someone had to be in charge, make the hard decisions.

And that person was Xavier, for better or worse. Val could step aside. This was still Xavier's office for three more months.

Laurel Dixon walked into the room and Xavier forgot about Val, LBC…his own name. Everything else in the world went dim. Except for her.

The woman following Adelaide looked nothing like

Marjorie, that was for sure. She looked nothing like any woman Xavier had ever met. Long, lush sable-colored hair hung down her back, but that only held his attention for a split second. Her face was arresting, with piercing silvery-gray eyes that locked onto his and wouldn't let go.

Something otherworldly passed between them and it was so fanciful a feeling that Xavier shook it off instantly. He didn't do *otherworldly*, whatever the hell that even meant. Never had he used such a term in his life to describe anything. But nothing else fit, and that made the whole encounter suspect. Besides, it was ridiculous to have any sort of reaction to a woman outside of desire, and even that was rarely strong enough for Xavier to note. Most, if not all, of his encounters with females could be described as mildly pleasurable, at best.

This woman had *trouble* written all over her if she could elicit such a response by merely walking into a room.

Coupled with the fact that she'd shown up without an appointment—Laurel Dixon raised his hackles about ten degrees past uncomfortable.

"Ms. Dixon." Val stood and offered his hand. "I'm Valentino LeBlanc, the director of LBC."

"Mr. LeBlanc. Very nice to meet you," she said, her clean voice vibrating across Xavier's skin with a force he couldn't shake.

He'd have said he preferred sultry voices. Sexy ones that purred when aroused. Laurel Dixon's voice could never be described as carnal, but that didn't seem to matter. He instantly wanted to hear it again. It was the kind of voice he could listen to for an hour and never get bored.

This was supposed to be an interview. Not a seduction. Actually, he'd never been seduced before, at least, not that he could recall. Usually he was the one making all the moves and he wasn't all that keen to be on the receiving end with a woman who wasn't even supposed to be here.

"Xavier LeBlanc," he announced and cleared his inexplicably ragged throat. "Current director of LBC. Val is just passing through."

She flicked her attention from Val to Xavier. This was the part where he had to stand and stick his hand out. Laurel Dixon clasped it, and when no lightning bolts forked between them, he relaxed an iota. That's when he made the mistake of letting his gaze rest on her lips. They curved up into a smile and *that* kicked him in the gut so hard, he felt it in his toes. Yanking his hand free, he sank back into his chair, wondering when, exactly, he'd lost his marbles.

"Two for the price of one," she said with a laugh that was just as arresting as her face. "I applaud the fact that you have such different hairstyles. Makes it easier to tell you apart."

Automatically he ran a hand over his closely cropped hair. He wore it that way because it looked professional. The style suited him and the fact that Val's too-long hair marked him as the rebel twin only worked in Xavier's favor. "Val gets lost on the way to the barber."

Despite the fact that he hadn't meant it as a joke, that made her laugh again, which pretty much solidified his resolve to stop talking. The less she laughed like that, the better.

"We weren't expecting you," Val said conversationally and indicated the seat next to him, then waited until Laurel slid into it before taking his own. "Though we're impressed with your enthusiasm. Right, Xavier?"

Figured that the second after he'd vowed to shut his mouth, Val dragged him right back into the conversation.

"That's one way to put it," he muttered. "I would have liked to schedule an interview."

"Oh, well, of course that would have been the appropriate thing to do," she admitted with an eye roll that shouldn't have been as appealing as it was. "But I'm so very interested in the job that I didn't want to leave anything to chance. So I thought, why wait?"

Why, indeed? "What about directing a food pantry excites you so much?"

"Oh, all of it," she answered quickly. "I love to help people in need and what better way than through one of the most basic fundamentals? Food is a necessity. I want to feed people."

"Well said," Val murmured.

Since his brother could have written that speech word for word, Xavier wasn't surprised he'd been moved by her passion. It sounded a little too memorized to Xavier's ear, and his gut had been screaming at him from the moment he'd first handed Val Laurel Dixon's résumé.

Something about her was off. He didn't like her. Nor did he like the way she unsettled him. If he had to constantly brace himself to be in her presence, how could they work together?

"Your experience is on the sparse side," Xavier said and tapped the résumé between them. "What did you do at the women's shelter that will segue into a services manager at a food pantry?"

Laurel launched into a well-rehearsed spiel about her role, highlighting her project management skills, and wrapped it up by getting into a spirited back-and-forth with Val about some of her ideas for new outreach.

His brother was sold on Laurel Dixon. Xavier could tell. Val had smiled through the entire exchange. Sure enough, after the candidate left, Val crossed his arms and said, "She's the one."

"She is so not the one."

"What? Why not?" Val dismissed that with a wave without waiting for an answer. "She's perfect."

"Then you hire her. In three months. I'm still in charge here and I say I want a different candidate."

"You're being stubborn for no reason," Val shot back, and some of the goodwill that had sprung up between them as they navigated the Great Inheritance Switch—as Xavier had been calling it in his head—began to slide away.

His caution had nothing to do with stubbornness

and he had plenty of reasons. "She's got no experience."

"Are you kidding? Everything she did at the women's shelter translates. Maybe not as elegantly as you might like, but you only have to deal with her for three months. After that, I'll be the one stuck with her if she's the wrong candidate. Humor me."

Xavier crossed his arms. "There's something not quite right about Laurel Dixon. I can't put my finger on it. You didn't sense that, too?"

"No. She's articulate and enthusiastic." The look Val shot him was part sarcasm and part pity. "Are you sure you're not picking up on the fact that she's not an emotionless robot like you?"

Ha. As if he hadn't heard that one before. But obviously Val had no clue about what really went on beneath Xavier's skin. Xavier just had a lot of practice at hiding what was going on inside. Edward LeBlanc had frowned on weakness, and in his mind, emotions and weakness went hand in hand.

"Yeah, that must be it."

Val rolled his eyes at Xavier's refusal to engage. "This is not the corporate world. We don't hire people based on how well they rip apart their prey here in nonprofit land. You need someone to replace Marjorie, like, yesterday. Unless you have a line of other options hidden away in the potato closet, you've got your new hire."

The damage was done. Now Xavier couldn't readily discount Laurel Dixon as a candidate, though the barb had hit its mark in a wholly different way than

Val probably even realized. No, this wasn't the corporate world and his raging uncertainty might well be rearing its ugly head here.

His father had done a serious number on him with this switcheroo. Xavier was only just coming to realize how many chunks of his confidence were missing as a result. How much of his inability to take an applicant at face value had to do with that?

Everything was suspect as a result.

"I'll deal with Laurel Dixon if that pleases your majesty," he told Val. "But I'm telling you up front. I don't trust her. She's hiding something and if it comes back to bite you, I'm going to remind you of this conversation."

Odds were good it was going to come back to bite Xavier long before it affected Val, who would leave to go back to the world of sane, logical, corporate politics in a few minutes. Xavier, on the other hand, would be working side by side for the next three months with a new services manager who made his skin hum when he looked at her.

He had a feeling he'd be spending a lot of time avoiding Laurel Dixon in order to protect himself, because that was what he did. No one was allowed to get under his skin and no one got an automatic place on Xavier's list of people he trusted.

Hopefully she liked hard work and thrived on opportunities to prove herself. Xavier was going to give her both.

Two

When Laurel Dixon had decided to go undercover at the LeBlanc Charities food pantry to investigate claims of fraud, she maybe should have picked a different position than services manager. Who would have thought they'd actually hire her, though?

They were supposed to admire her enthusiasm and give her a lesser position. One that gave her plenty of access to the people she needed to interview on the down low and plenty of time to do it. Instead, she'd been handed the keys to the kingdom—which should have put her in a great place to dig into LBC's books. Donors needed to know that LBC wasn't on the up-and-up, that they were only pretending to help people in need while the thieves lined their own pockets.

Except thus far she'd had zero time to even think about how to expose the charity's fraudulent practices.

Of course, a lot of that had to do with one infuriating man named Xavier LeBlanc.

Just because he arrived at LBC at the ungodly hour of 6:00 a.m. and worked through lunch didn't mean the rest of the world had to do the same. But they'd all done it, Laurel included, though she didn't suffer from the same sense of anxiety the other staffers seemed to feel around their interim boss.

But what was she supposed to do, stroll in at nine and draw attention to herself? She'd taken this job under false pretenses. And she couldn't back out now.

Ugh. This was what she got for trying a whole different approach to investigative reporting. This was supposed to be her big breakthrough story. The one that would fix her reputation in the industry while appealing to her sense of fair play and her drive to help people at the same time. If she went undercover, surely she could get the facts for the exposé, and this time, there would be no embarrassing counter-story exposing the lack of foundation for her accusations.

Embarrassing and nearly career killing. Thanks to social media shares and the eternal stores of video, her blunder would never be forgotten. But she could give her audience something else to play with. As long as she didn't make a single mistake with this investigation. When she blew the whistle on LBC, it would be career *making*. A triumph that would erase the mistakes of her last investigation.

Or so she'd laid out in a foolproof mental plan that ended up having a remarkable number of holes.

Instead, she'd spent her first few hours on the job following Adelaide around as the admin explained how Xavier envisioned things working around LBC—and how fast he expected Laurel to get it that way. Apparently, the old manager, Marjorie, had left operations in a bit of disarray when she'd left, but Mr. LeBlanc couldn't be bothered to tell her his expectations himself.

At one o'clock, she'd had enough.

Feigning hunger and fatigue, she begged off from Adelaide's cheerful tour of the facility and bearded the lion in his den. She didn't mind hard work, but only if there was a distinct payoff, and so far, she hadn't seen one. It was time to shake things up.

Xavier LeBlanc glanced up at her sharp knock, his deep blue eyes registering not one iota of surprise or curiosity—nothing. It was a great trick, one she wished she knew how to replicate. It would come in handy as she pretended she knew what the hell she was doing at this new gig.

In lieu of that, she'd settle for a mentor who could give her the insight she needed.

"Got a minute?" she asked and didn't wait for the answer. He would see her whether he liked it or not. How was she supposed to figure out who was responsible for the fraud inside these walls if she didn't keep the man in charge very, very close?

His gaze tracked her as she waltzed right into his

office with confidence. He seemed like the type who wouldn't appreciate a mousey approach.

"What can I do for you?" he asked, his sinfully sexy voice rumbling in his chest.

She missed a step. His sexiness quotient really shouldn't be something she noticed. At all. Xavier LeBlanc wasn't allowed to be sexy. He was her boss and she'd been hired based on a lie. One she'd told with good reason, and all of the experience on her résumé was real. But still.

None of that equaled free rein to be attracted to the man behind the desk. And none of that stopped her insides from quivering as his gaze slid down her face to her mouth. He'd done that in the interview more than once and she'd blown it off then. She thought she'd been mistaken. That they'd been stray looks that didn't mean anything. She'd imagined it.

Today? Punch in the girl parts.

She could no more pretend it hadn't happened than she could ignore it. Did Xavier have any clue how unsettling it was to have a man who looked like him slide his gaze to your mouth as if he couldn't decide how to kiss you? Not if. *How*. Because it was happening and he wanted you to anticipate it.

Okay, she had to ignore that. She had a job. Two jobs. Neither were going to go well if she didn't pull it together. Besides, he hadn't done or said anything inappropriate. Likely she was still imagining it.

"Adelaide is a sweet lady," Laurel began. "But I don't get the impression she's fully communicating your vision as well as I would hope. Would it be possible for you to be a little more hands-on?"

In a totally nonpervy way, of course, she added silently as the atmosphere in the room went dead still. Totally could have phrased that better. More professional. Less *I want you on this desk right now.*

Xavier's eyebrows lifted a fraction. "What, exactly, are you asking me to do?"

Oh, man. Surely he didn't mean for that to sound as leading as it did. But then, she'd started it. Was he expecting her to finish it?

Her mind immediately filled in those blanks with several things she could ask him to do. Curiosity was both her strength and her biggest weakness, and she almost never hesitated to investigate things she was dying to know, like whether Xavier's shoulders felt as strong and broad as they looked and how he planned to kiss her.

Of course, she'd never say that out loud. She couldn't. Well, okay, she totally *could* and she had a feeling Xavier would deliver. But she wouldn't. It was highly unethical, for more reasons than one.

But she couldn't get the sudden and sharp images out of her head of what might happen if she did take the hint in his voice and really laid out what she might like. Nothing wrong with a little harmless fantasizing about a sexy man, was there?

"I, um…" *Voice too husky. Not professional. Focus.* She cleared her throat. "It's my first day. I was hoping you and I might talk about your expectations."

Good. That didn't sound like the lead-in to a seduction scene at all.

"I expect you to manage the operations of this charity," he said succinctly. "Nothing more, nothing less."

"I got that part." Sexy, but either Xavier was obtuse or he had way more confidence in her than he had a right to. "But this is your vision I'm executing. I don't know anything about you or your ideas for how things should work. Tell me what my typical day should look like."

Xavier lifted his hands from the keyboard of his laptop and laced them together in a deliberately precise gesture that had the mark of a man demonstrating his patience. His hands were strong and capable, with long lean fingers that she had to stop envisioning on her body.

"That's what I asked Adelaide to do. If she's failing to—"

"No, no." *God*, no. The last thing she'd intended to do was put a spotlight on Adelaide. The poor woman probably had nightmares about Xavier as it was. "She's great. Very helpful. But I want to hear it straight from you. We're going to be working very closely together, after all."

"We're doing nothing of the kind. I hired you to be invisible and ensure that I never have to think about the operations of this place."

Oh. That was not going to work. Laurel leaned forward and laced her own hands together near the edge of the desk, mirroring his pose. "See, that's exactly that sort of thing that Adelaide could never convey. She showed me where departments are and introduced me to people. But I need the mind of Xavier LeBlanc to mesh with mine so we're in sync. Tell me what you'd do. That's the best way to ensure you don't have to think about things, because I will instantly know how you'd want something handled."

And that philosophy had the added bonus of filling in the gaps of her skill set, not to mention allowing her to grill him on how much he knew about the fraud. Her sources had been volunteers in the food pantry and they had given her several credible tips about substitutions that didn't make it into the books, among other things. What she already knew was likely the tip of the iceberg. In her line of work, there was always more to discover.

But she needed to know how high up it went, if Xavier knew about it or if this strange and unexplained switch between the brothers had removed the real culprit from LBC.

Maybe the mysterious switch had its roots in the fraud. She had to know.

At the same time, she couldn't make mistakes. If Xavier's brother had spearheaded or approved the fraud, she had to find proof. Of course, it could have started with Xavier's reign, which added to the complexity of the investigation. It was a wrinkle she hadn't seen coming but adhering to Xavier's directive to be "invisible" wasn't going to reveal even a tiny slice of what she needed to uncover.

Xavier's gaze skittered over hers again and she

had the distinct impression he didn't quite know what to do with her. Good. An off-kilter man spilled secrets he meant to keep close to the vest. She relaxed a smidgen. This undercover business couldn't be too hard. Or, rather, she couldn't allow it to be. This story was too important to the people LBC should be serving instead of cheating. The story was too important to her career.

"Here's what I want, Ms. Dixon." His low voice snaked through her and she tried really hard not to react, but she didn't have his ability to be stone-faced. Neither did he miss her reaction, absorbing it with a long, slow pause laden with things unsaid. "I want you to ensure LBC operates smoothly enough that I can focus on fundraising. Outside of that, I don't care what you do."

She blinked. "Sure you do. You're in charge. Everything flows uphill, right?"

That was the core of an investigative reporter's philosophy, the one they taught in Digging for Facts 101. Follow the money. The guy in the corner office was always the place to start because he made all the decisions. If anything illegal was going on, it usually went all the way to the top.

Of course, this situation had the added layer of the guy at the top not being the normal guy. All at once, she hoped Xavier would be in the clear and she'd instead be taking down his brother. Which would be a shame, because she'd genuinely liked Val.

She couldn't let her personal feelings compromise the investigation, as they had in her last story. She couldn't afford to *like* anyone in this situation.

"Indeed it does," Xavier finally said.

His gaze still hadn't left hers, and if she hadn't known better, she'd have thought he might be fighting some of the same attraction she was. Surely he had his pick of women. He wasn't trying to be sexy as a come-on; it was just a natural part of who he was and she didn't for a second think he'd turned it on specifically for her.

"Great, then we're on the same page. You're in charge and I'm here to execute your orders. What would you like me to do first?"

"Explain why it seems like you're flirting with me."

Laurel's lungs seized and she choked on a breath. Tears leaked from her eyes as she coughed, and if she was really lucky, mascara streaks were even now forming below her lashes.

"What?" she asked when she recovered. "I'm not flirting with you."

If anything, he was the one exuding all the come-hither vibes. At times, it was so strong, she was barely hanging on by the fingernails.

His implacable expression didn't change. "Good. It would be a bad idea to get involved."

Oh, well, *that* was a telling statement. Not "You're not my type." Not "You've mistaken me for a heterosexual." *Bad idea to get involved.* That meant he felt all the sizzle, too.

Interesting.

How much closer could she get to Xavier LeBlanc

and would that benefit her story? Or simply benefit *her*? The man knew his way around an orgasm—she could tell. And while this exposé lay at the pinnacle of her personal goals, she couldn't help but want to investigate her reaction to Xavier as a man.

She had a core-deep desire to *know* things, and at this moment, Xavier topped the list.

"A bad, bad idea," she repeated and crossed her fingers behind her back. "I solemnly swear that I will refrain from all double entendres, loaded statements and anything that could be construed as flirting while you and I are working so closely together."

"I didn't say we'd be working closely together," he corrected, and all at once she wondered what it would take to get him well and truly rattled to the point of revealing something unintended.

If she hoped to dig up enough dirt for an exposé, she'd have to figure it out. Everyone had their tipping point and people had spilled secrets to her in the past, often before realizing it. Usually that happened after she'd gained a measure of their trust, though.

How ethical was it to seduce it out of someone? She'd never tried that particular method before and there was no way to deny the idea excited her. Which meant it really was a bad idea. But still viable. She needed more information before fully committing.

"Oh, come on. We just hashed that out. You're in charge, I'm here to do exactly what you say but not sexually and we're both going to ignore the chemistry. Where, exactly, did I lose you, Mr. LeBlanc?"

At that, he actually laughed, and the heavy, rich

sound did flippy things to her insides. His deep blue eyes speared her and she got all caught up in him in a very nonprofessional way. Yeah, there might not be a whole lot of choice in the matter and she might not be the one doing the seducing. It was delicious to contemplate, either way.

"I'm not lost. Just…reassessing," he said.

"That sounds promising. Why don't you share your vision with me, at least, and we'll take it from there?"

"Vision for what?"

He'd leaned into the space between them and she was having a hard time concentrating. Xavier had a very potent presence that had latched onto her skin in a wholly disturbing way. "For, um, LBC. As a charity. What's the vision? Mission statement? That kind of thing."

"Feed people," he stated bluntly. "What more is there?"

"A lot. At the shelter, our goal was to give women back some control in their lives. Provide them with choices. The shelter part was just one of the mechanisms we employed."

That had been satisfying work, even as a means to an end as she put herself through college. Sure, she'd had to fudge the dates a little on her résumé and leave off the last few years of employment so no one knew she'd worked for a news channel—which had subsequently fired her. But her drive to help people through knowledge hadn't changed. She still believed in the value of nonprofit organizations, particularly those that served people at the poverty line.

That's why it was so important to expose the fraud here. The money funneling through this organization should go to the people who came through the doors in need, not toward lining someone's pocket because they saw an easy way to skim profits.

Xavier's face turned to granite, which was his default more often than not. "You seem to forget I'm just filling in. This is not my normal world."

All at once, the information she craved had nothing to do with LBC and everything to do with Xavier LeBlanc himself. He was such a fascinating puzzle who gave very little away. She wanted to unlock him in the worst way. "But your brother mentioned that your mother started this charity fifteen years ago. Surely you've been involved to some degree."

"What you see is the sole extent of my involvement." He waved at the desk. "This is where I'll sit for three more months, and in that time I need to hold the best fundraiser this place has ever had. Mission statements are not my concern."

She blinked, but his expression didn't change. He was serious. Okay, wow.

"You're going to have a very big problem, then. People don't give money to fundraisers. They give to a cause they believe in. Your job is to make them believe in it. Don't you think that in a city like Chicago there are a hundred—a *thousand*—places for people to donate? How do they decide? You help them decide by passionately pitching your mission statement to them."

"I'll take that under advisement." In the long

pause, they stared at each other without blinking. "You've done fundraising before. Did you apply for the wrong position here?"

Yes. Yes, she had.

That was all the opening she needed to segue this potential disaster into something more her speed. "Perhaps, but only because you posted a job opening for the wrong position. Sounds like you need someone in your back pocket to tell you what to do, not the other way around. Were you not aware that you have serious deficiencies in your operating philosophy?"

Xavier leaned back in his chair as his gaze narrowed. "Can I be honest with you, Ms. Dixon?"

Oh, God, yes. Please spill all your secrets, Mr. LeBlanc.

"Only if you call me Laurel."

His lips lifted into a brief smile that she fully expected meant he was about to argue with her. But he didn't. "Laurel, then. You need to understand what's happening here and I'm choosing to trust you, which is not something I do lightly."

His tone or his smile or her own conscience tripped something inside. Guilt plowed through her stomach out of nowhere. It was one thing to dig deep enough to learn someone's secrets when they were scamming, but she had no evidence Xavier was even involved in the fraud. What if her investigation caused problems for him?

Ugh, she was getting way ahead of herself. Her sources were credible and if there was something to uncover, Xavier would likely be happy that she'd done so. It was a public service, really. Surely he'd respect that.

"I'll do my best to be worthy of that trust."

He nodded once. "Then I have a confession. I am not well versed in how to run a charity. I do need help."

She very nearly rolled her eyes. This was him being honest? "I already figured that out."

"I'm doing my best to keep that nugget of truth from the rest of the staff," he said wryly. "Which is why I try to stay out of their areas of expertise. That's where you come in."

"I hear you. You want to hide out here in the office while everyone else does the dirty work." She stared him down as his eyebrows came together. "Too bad. You signed up to run LBC. Now do it. I'll help. We'll be partners."

She stuck out her hand and waited. She needed him, whether she liked it or not. Whether *he* liked it or not. And the reverse was also clearly true. They would do this together or not at all. If she had a partner, the less chance she had of screwing up.

Xavier let her sweat it for about thirty seconds and then reluctantly reached out to clasp her hand for a very long beat that neither of them mistook for a simple handshake. There was too much electricity, too much unsaid for that.

The less she let him focus on that, the better.

Three

Partners.

That was a concept Xavier liked a whole lot, given his distinct impression that Laurel Dixon was hiding something. He liked it even better that she'd been the one to suggest working together. The closer he kept her, the easier it would be to keep an eye on her.

He trusted her about as much as he'd trust a convicted car thief with the keys to his Aston Martin.

But he also understood that his lack of trust wasn't specific to Laurel. If he really wanted to get honest about it, his inability to stop being both suspicious and cautious had probably been at least half of Marjorie's problem with him. That's why he'd thought a hands-off approach with the new services manager might work best. Not to mention the fact that he couldn't shake that weird, misty feeling that sprang up inside whenever he was in the same room with Laurel Dixon. He'd hoped to avoid examining that by staying away from her.

Ms. Dixon had blown that plan to smithereens.

Jury was still out on how much wreckage he'd have to step over. Especially given the instant and volatile chemistry between them, which he'd been wholly prepared to pretend didn't exist until she'd so eloquently refused to let him. So that was a thing. The next three months should be incredibly taxing and exceedingly painful, then.

"Partners. What happens next?" Xavier asked Laurel once he'd dropped her hand, though the severed contact didn't eliminate the buzzing awareness arcing between them at all.

Not that he'd expected it to. Regardless of what he called the vibe between them, it wasn't going away. The trick was managing it. Which meant it would be a bad idea to touch her again, and of course, that was all he could think about.

"Follow me."

She slid from the seat she'd perched in when she first came into his office and glanced over her shoulder, perhaps to ensure he was doing as she commanded. As if he'd miss a second of whatever she had up her sleeve. Not likely.

Xavier trailed her to the receptionist's desk. Adelaide's eyes widened behind her bifocals as they approached and taut lines appeared around the woman's mouth. He nearly growled at her just to see if she'd actually come out of her skin. What good was it to have people afraid of him if he couldn't have fun with it occasionally?

Before he could try it, Laurel flipped a lock of her long sable-colored hair behind her back. "Today is your lucky day, Addy. You're in charge from now on. Mr. LeBlanc has given you a promotion."

"I did not. *Oof.*" Laurel's elbow glanced off his ribs, leaving a sharp, smarting circle of *shut up* below his heart. "I mean…yeah. What Laurel said."

Adelaide's wide-eyed gaze flitted back and forth between the two of them as if she couldn't quite get her bearings. He knew the feeling.

"That's very generous, Mr. LeBlanc," she squeaked. "But I don't understand. A promotion?"

"Exactly." Laurel beamed so brightly, Xavier could see the rays from his position behind her. "To Services Manager. You're going to take Marjorie's place."

Wait, what? That was going a little far. If Adelaide had been remotely qualified or interested in the position, she would have applied for it the second the job posting had gone up. What, exactly, was Laurel up to?

"Are you sure about this?" he muttered in Laurel's ear and caught her elbow a hairbreadth from his ribs, holding it tight just in case she was stronger than she looked.

Clearly she had a plan and intended for Xavier to follow it. The elbow to the ribs indicated that if he wanted to have a conversation about her tactics, she'd indulge him later.

"You know everything about this place, Adelaide. Tell Mr. LeBlanc," Laurel instructed with a nauseating amount of cheer. "You gave me such a thorough tour of the place that I thought it would never end. There's not a nook or cranny at LBC that you don't have some sort of insight into. Is there?"

Obediently, Adelaide shook her head. "No, ma'am. I've been here seven years and started in the kitchen as a volunteer. I love every last board and nail in this place."

"I could tell." Laurel jerked her head at Xavier. "Mr. LeBlanc was just bemoaning the fact that he didn't have anyone to help organize a fundraiser that LBC so desperately needs."

Oh, dear God. That was not what he'd said. *At all.* But before he could correct the grievous misrepresentation that gave everyone the impression he was being a big baby about the tasks laid out for him, Laurel rushed on.

"I figured, this is Addy's opportunity to really make a difference. Step up and show us all what she's made of. You just do what Marjorie did and that'll leave me free to help Mr. LeBlanc get some money flowing in. Are you good with that?"

When Adelaide smiled and clapped her hands like she'd just been given the biggest Christmas present, Xavier's mouth fell open. Hastily, he closed it before anyone figured out that Laurel Dixon had just shocked the hell out of him. He didn't shock easily, and it was even harder to remember the last time he'd been unable to control his expression.

The two women went back and forth on the logistics for a furious couple of minutes until Xavier couldn't take it any longer.

"So, that's it?" he interrupted. "Adelaide, you can do what Marjorie did and everyone's good with that?"

Both women swiveled to stare at him. Laurel raised a brow. "Sorry, did we lose you again? Yes. Adelaide is in charge. She'll do a fantastic job."

Xavier should have asked more questions back in his office, like whether *partner* meant something different where Laurel had come from. When she'd thrown out the idea that they'd be working closely together, he'd reassessed his idea of how their interaction might go. And he'd come to the conclusion that perhaps she *could* come to him for approval on the budget, or maybe to get his help vetting new volunteers. That sort of thing.

He had not once suggested that she sign herself up to take over his inheritance test. That was *his*. He needed to prove to his father—and himself—that he could and would handle anything the old man threw at him. Ten million dollars was a cheap price to pay in order to get back on even ground, regain his confidence and lose the edge of vulnerability he'd been carrying since the reading of the will.

No one was allowed to get in the way of that.

"Excuse us, please," he said to Adelaide through gritted teeth.

Pulling Laurel back into his office, he shut the

door and leaned on it, half afraid she'd find a way to open it again despite the hundred and seventy-five pounds of man holding it shut.

Instantly, he realized his mistake.

Laurel's presence filled the room, blanketing him with that otherworldly, mystical nonsense that he couldn't think through.

"What the hell was all that about?" he demanded and couldn't find a shred of remorse at how rough it came out. "You shuffled off all your duties to Adelaide—without asking, by the way. What, exactly, are you going to be doing?"

"Helping you, of course." She patted his arm and the contact sang through his flesh clear to the bone. "We have a fundraiser to organize. Which I'm pretty sure is what I just said."

The trap had been laid so neatly that he still hadn't quite registered whether the teeth had closed around his ankle or not. "You don't have enough experience fundraising."

She shrugged. "I do have *some*. What's your hang-up about experience? Adelaide doesn't have any experience." She accompanied that statement with air quotes. "But she's been learning on the job for years by following Marjorie around. She'll do great."

"Running a charity takes an iron fist," he shot back instantly. "Not an owl face and a lot of head nodding."

Laurel just laughed. "Owl face? Better not let her hear that. Women who wear glasses don't take kindly to name-calling."

"I didn't mean——" The headache brewing behind his eyes spread to his temples. "I called her an owl because she just stands there and looks wise. Instead of telling people what to do. I— Never mind."

Laurel Dixon had officially driven him around the bend. And now Adelaide had just been given a promotion that she seemed super pleased with. He couldn't take it away, though likely he'd have to spend a lot of time following *her* around to make sure she didn't drive operations into the ground. Hiring Laurel had been one thing, because at least he could blame that on Val if it didn't work out, but this was a whole other mess.

One he had no graceful way of undoing without upsetting the admin. Or Laurel, who might do God knew what as her next trick.

"Okay. Fine," he ground out. "Adelaide is Marjorie. She's going to be great. You're going to help with fundraising. Are you going to be great, too?"

"Of course."

She flipped a lock of hair over her shoulder again, and he couldn't help but wonder why she wore it down when her hands were constantly fiddling with it. She should wear it up. Then he wouldn't be tempted to put his own hands through it just to see if it felt as satiny and lush as it looked.

He crossed his arms. No point in tempting fate. "Fantastic. What's the plan, General?"

"Nicknames already?" Her long eyelashes swept her cheeks as she treated him to a very long, pointed once-over that lingered in inappropriate places. "I thought that wouldn't happen until much later in our association. Under…different circumstances."

In bed, she meant. The implication was clear. And he definitely shouldn't be feeling the spark of her suggestion in those inappropriate places. "It fit. Can't help it."

"Don't worry. I like it." The atmosphere in the office got a whole lot heavier as she stared at him. "And I like that you've already clued in that I don't sit around and wait for things to happen to me."

"I knew that a half second after Adelaide told me you were here for an interview that I hadn't arranged," he told her bluntly. "You're an easy read."

Something flitted through her gaze. A shadow. He couldn't put his finger on what she had going on beneath the surface, but that gut deep feeling told him again she had something to hide.

How many secrets might she spill if he did take her into his bed?

Once that thought formed, he couldn't stop thinking about it. He wasn't like that, not normally. But Laurel had barreled right through what he'd call his *normal* and redefined everything. Maybe he needed to return the favor.

"I'm pretty transparent," she agreed readily, but another layer dropped into place over her expression.

She was a terrible liar. Or perhaps he was just incredibly tuned in to her, which didn't seem to have a downside. Other than the one where he'd just been boxed into a corner and had no graceful way to avoid spending a lot of time in her company.

"I probably see more than you'd like," he told her, and she blinked. This was a fun game. "For example, I'm pretty sure that you just maneuvered yourself into a position as my fundraising assistant because you can't stay away from me."

He didn't believe that for a second, but he definitely wanted to hear what she'd say to counter it.

Her eyebrows inched up toward her hairline and she relaxed an iota. "Well, that's a provocative statement. What if I said it's true?"

Then she'd be lying again. She had a whole other agenda, one he hadn't figured out yet, but if she wanted to work it like the attraction between them got top billing, he could play along. "I'd say we have a problem, then. We can't get involved. It would be too…sticky."

Her lips curved at his choice of words, as intended. "That's a shame. I'm a fan of sticky."

"Stickiness is for candy." All at once, a very distinct image sprang into his head of her on his desk naked with a caramel melting on her tongue. His whole body went stiff. "I like it best when things are uncomplicated."

At that, she snorted, moving in to lay a hand on his arm in the exact opposite of what this back-off conversation had been intended to convey. He'd wanted to catch her off guard but so far she'd held her own.

Reluctant admiration for this woman warred with bone-deep desire and flat-out irritation.

"Please," she muttered with a sarcastic grin as

she squeezed his forearm. "You're the least uncomplicated man I've ever met. At least do me the courtesy of being honest about the fact that you're not attracted to me, if that's what's going on."

Oh, nicely played. She'd put the ball firmly in his court. He could take the out and claim he didn't feel the heavy arousal that she could almost assuredly see for herself, giving her the opportunity to call him out as a liar. Or he could admit that she made him hotter than asphalt in a heat wave and call a truce.

He went with option three: ensuring she fully understood he didn't dance to her tune.

"I don't think honesty is on the table here. Do you?"

The atmosphere splintered as she stiffened, but to her credit, she kept a smile on her face. "Touché. We'll go back to ignoring the chemistry, then."

"That's best." And not at all what he'd been talking about, but he also hadn't expected her to voluntarily blurt out her secrets. All in good time. "Now, about this fundraiser…"

"Oh, right." Her hand dropped away from his arm—finally—and she got a contemplative look as if she really had given away her job with the intent of diving into his hell with gusto. "We should attend someone else's fundraiser and take notes."

"That's—" he blinked "—a really good idea."

One he should have thought of. That's what he'd do in the diamond trenches. If another jewelry outlet had a strategy he liked, he'd study it. Why not apply the same to charity?

Laurel smiled, putting some sparkle in her silver-gray eyes. "I'll start researching some possibilities and then we'll take a field trip."

Fantastic. If he couldn't stay away from Laurel, then he'd settle for spending as much time in her company as he could until he figured out her agenda. If it was merely to indulge in their impossible-to-ignore chemistry, then he might find a way to be on board with that, as long as he could protect what was his at the same time.

Jury was still out on just how difficult she'd make it.

Four

By Friday, Adelaide had Xavier's vote of confidence. She really had been studying at Marjorie's side for quite some time, showing off a deep knowledge of all things LBC, and she made sound decisions without a lot of deliberation. The staff responded to her as if she'd always been in charge, and he liked her style.

Not that he'd tell her that. She managed to convey a fair amount of dislike for him with pretty much every word out of her mouth and sometimes without saying anything at all. It was impressive.

But it felt like LBC was running smoothly for the first time in forever. Since Marjorie had dropped her set of keys on his desk with a clank and turned on her heel. Maybe even before that. So he gave Adelaide a pass on the disdain. She didn't have to like him as long as she did her job so he could do his. Or, at least, pretend to do his until he figured out how to turn the tide in his favor.

Laurel poked her head through his partially opened office door, sable hair swinging. "Why am I not surprised to find you behind your desk?"

"Because this is where I work?" he offered blithely.

In the week since he and Laurel had become "partners," he'd learned that he had almost no shot at responding to a question like that to her satisfaction. He'd given up trying and went with the most obvious answer.

She made a noise with her tongue that could easily be mistaken for a ticking clock. "Because you're hiding now that Addy has it all under control, more likely."

He lifted a shoulder. "Must not be hiding well enough. You found me."

"I was looking for you." The rest of her body followed her head as she slid through the cracked door uninvited. "Probably I'm the only one who is, though."

"For a reason, one would hope," he shot back pointedly before she launched into yet another discussion about how he could do more to interact with the staff. Laurel's job had somehow morphed from Services Manager to Fundraising Assistant to Xavier's Keeper. He hadn't figured out yet how to veer her back into something a little less invasive. "I am actually doing paperwork."

If staring at paperwork counted, then it wasn't so much of a lie. Otherwise, he'd stopped doing paperwork an hour ago and instead had been stewing about the latest fundraising numbers.

He was short. A lot. He had less than three months to raise north of seven million dollars and the near impossibility of the task writhed in his stomach like a greasy eel. As a result, he'd spent a lot of time sorting through fundraising ideas on his own, which was something he'd outsource to Laurel over his dead body.

The trick was engaging her enough so that she *thought* she'd snowed him into this partnership, when in reality, he only let her have enough rope to bind them very closely together—strictly so he didn't miss whatever she had up her sleeve. Sharing the actual work with Laurel wasn't happening.

Thus far, she hadn't seemed to clue in. She barged into his office at her leisure to discuss what had become her pet project. He'd bet a hundred K that she'd spotted a notice in the society pages about the Art for Autism Association fundraiser tonight and she'd come by to announce she was dragging him along to it, pretending it wasn't a date when, in reality, it was a great excuse to spend the evening together without admitting she wanted to.

He'd put up some empty protests and eventually let her think she'd talked him into it. Getting out from underneath the eyes at LBC sounded like an opportune way to dig a little deeper into Laurel Dixon and whatever it was about her that niggled at his suspicions.

She curled her lip at the printed pages under his fingers, eyeing the black type as if she could actually read it from that distance. "Good thing for you I have something much more exciting to put on your agenda. You're taking me on a hot date tonight."

Oh, God, yes. The scene spilled through his mind without an ounce of prompting. Laurel in a little black dress—backless, of course, designed to make a man's mouth water—and sky-high heels that did amazing things to her legs. Her voice would be lowered enough to keep their conversation private. Hair down and brushed to a high gleam. She'd take his breath away the moment he opened the door and he'd never quite get his equilibrium back until maybe the next day…

What was he *thinking*?

Xavier sat back in his chair and crossed his arms with feigned nonchalance in case his initial—and so very inappropriate—response got too big to stay under his skin and started leaking out of his pores.

And this even though he'd *known* it was coming. It was just…she'd called it a date, after all, and in the process, uncovered his previously undiscovered craving to do it for real. What was he supposed to do with her?

Laurel was so much more dangerous than he'd credited.

"We're not dating." A token protest. It was only

a matter of time before he figured out how to keep his wits about him as he seduced the truth out of her. Meanwhile, he had to play it like he still planned to keep her at arm's length. All the balls they had in the air should be exhausting. "We've covered this."

Instead, it was invigorating.

She waved it off. "Yeah, yeah. This isn't a real date. You're taking me on a field trip. I found a great foundation doing a unique fundraiser. Tonight."

Pretending it was not a real date he could do. In fact, it got a righteous *hallelujah*. Silently, of course, but still. His arms relaxed and dropped into his lap. "Fantastic. Where?"

"Art gallery." She glanced at her watch, her attention already galloping away from this conversation into whatever else was going on in her brain. "I called as your representative and they were more than happy to take your money. The lady even sent a courier over with the tickets. I have to leave now so I can pick up a dress and get my hair done. I have reservations at LaGrange at eight. Meet me there."

Like hell. He did things the right way when it came to taking a woman to dinner. Especially one he wanted to keep close for more reasons than one. "We'll need time to strategize. I'll be at your house at seven thirty to pick you up."

Her eyebrows lifted and he couldn't help the smug sense of satisfaction that crept through him. Laurel wasn't so easy to surprise. He'd have to repeat that a whole bunch more, simply because he liked the idea of knocking her off balance before she did it to him.

"Well, then, I have to say yes to *strategizing*."

Innuendo dripped from her voice and the suggestion pinged around inside him, doing interesting things down below. He let the charged moment drag out because it suited him and then smiled. "Wear black."

"Duh. You, too," she suggested with a once-over that clearly said she found his jeans and T-shirt lacking in some way.

"I've been to my share of society events. I think I'm good." Finally, he'd have a chance to slip back into his old self, the one that wore three-thousand-dollar suits to the office as a matter of course. He could even pull his Yacht-Master out of the box in his closet. "See you at seven thirty."

She lifted her chin in amused acknowledgment that he'd won that round and took off to do whatever female rituals she'd lined up to get herself ready for tonight.

Xavier was dressed in his favorite tux by seven, but forced himself to cool his heels. Laurel did not need any ammunition, and showing up early would clue her in as to how much he'd been anticipating this not-a-date—and not just because he had an agenda of his own for the evening. He wanted to see her.

Labels were simply a mechanism to drive them both toward what they wanted using acceptable parameters. They'd be spending the evening together in formal wear, eating dinner and attending an art show, all of which could lead to something very good. Sure, it was pitched as an opportunity to scout out how another charity did fundraising, but they were both adults who shared a sizzling attraction.

There was no reason he couldn't enjoy the results of seducing her, even if his motives weren't entirely pure. Women who hid things didn't get to be self-righteous about how their secrets came to light.

Besides, if she hadn't wanted to play with fire, she'd have picked a fundraising field trip with a lot fewer matches. Like the 5k run through Highland Park that the Chicago Children's Advocacy Center had on tap for tomorrow. No chance to get the slightest bit cozy in the middle of the day while sweating your butt off. Probably that's what they should have signed up for.

But he had to be honest and admit that he liked a good fire, himself. As long as he was the one controlling the flame.

The moment he rang Laurel's doorbell at 7:31, she swung it open as if she'd been standing there waiting. Clearly *she* had no qualms about letting him know she'd been eagerly anticipating his arrival. And then his brain registered the woman. Whatever illusion he'd cooked up that had given him the idea he might have the slightest iota of control vanished like smoke in a hurricane.

Holy hell. "Laurel…"

His brain couldn't form coherent sentences after that. She was so far past gorgeous that she bordered on ethereal. Angelic. Something a man with far more poetry in his soul than Xavier LeBlanc would have to immortalize because all he could think was *wow*.

Black was Laurel's color. There was something about it that paired with her skin and eyes to make both luminous. The dress was exactly the right length to be considered modest, but also to make a man wishful. And her stilettos—sexy enough to make his teeth ache along with the rest of his body.

"I got lucky," she said with a laugh, like everything was fine and his entire world hadn't just been knocked from its axis. "This was the first dress I tried on and the price tag wasn't the equivalent of my mortgage."

"It's…" *Perfect*. But his tongue went numb. He swallowed. What the hell was wrong with him? It was just a dress. With a woman inside it. He'd participated in hundreds of similar scenarios where he'd picked up a date at her door.

But none of them had ever intrigued him as much as this one. None of them had irritated him beyond the point of reason. None of them had caught him off guard as many times in a row as Laurel. None of them had stirred something inside that he couldn't explain or even fully acknowledge.

It was far past time to stop ignoring it and start figuring out how to deal with it.

Because he still didn't trust her. No matter what. He couldn't think of her as a hot date or he'd never regain an ounce of control—and he needed control to get through the evening. She was his companion for a fundraising research trip. Nothing more.

"You look great," he said and cleared his throat.

That husky quality in his voice would not do. "If you're ready?"

He extended a hand toward the limousine at her curb and waited as she locked the door behind her, then he followed her down the sidewalk, trying to keep his eyes off her extremely nice rear. The dress wasn't backless but it did dip down into a V beneath her hair, which she had worn down. She didn't seem to ever put it up, which he appreciated. Hair like hers should never be hidden in a ponytail or bun.

And he'd veered right back into thinking of her as a woman instead of his partner in all things fund-raising. The problem was that she wasn't really his partner and he didn't want her in that role. But he had to do *something* with her now that she'd shuffled off daily operations to Adelaide, if for no other reason than because Val liked her and had asked Xavier to keep her around. Dinner and an art show it was, then.

The atmosphere in the limo bordered on electric, and he cursed the fact that he'd specifically instructed his staff to skip the champagne because this wasn't a date. It would have been nice to have something to occupy his hands.

Come on. You're better than this.

"LaGrange is an interesting restaurant choice," he said more smoothly than his still-tingling tongue should have allowed. "A favorite?"

Laurel shrugged, drawing attention to her bare shoulders. They were creamy and flawless, like her long legs. This field trip was either the worst idea ever conceived or sheer brilliance. He couldn't decide which.

"I've never been able to score a table there, but oddly enough, when I throw your name around, people jump." She winked. "Don't judge, but I'm enjoying my ride on the Xavier LeBlanc train."

Hell on a horse. The train hadn't even left the station yet and she was already impressed? He bit back forty-seven provocative responses about what else might be in store for a woman on his arm and opted for what hopefully passed as a smile. "I know the owner of LaGrange. Not everyone jumps when I say jump."

"I don't believe that for a second," she murmured. "You seem like the type who takes no prisoners. Tell me about running LeBlanc Jewelers. I bet you're magnificent in the boardroom."

As ego strokes went, that one could have done some damage, but he'd caught the slightly off-color tinge to her tone. She was fishing for something. That alone put an interesting spin on the conversation. He couldn't help but indulge her, mostly to see if he could trip her up enough to spill bits of her agenda.

"I'm magnificent in every room." He let that sink in, gratified by her instant half smile that said she caught the innuendo. "But in the boardroom, I do my job. Nothing more."

"So modest. I read up on LeBlanc Jewelers. It's almost a billion-dollar company, up nearly 20 percent since you took over five years ago. That's impressive."

The reminder tripped some not-so-pleasant internal stuff that he'd rather not dwell on tonight. "Again. That's my job. If I didn't do it well, the board wouldn't let me keep it. What about you? Once we organize a fundraiser for LBC and I go back to LeBlanc Jewelers, what do you envision yourself doing?"

Val wouldn't keep her in the role of fundraiser, or, at least, Xavier didn't think he would. Honestly, he didn't know what Val might do and that was at least half Xavier's problem. The inner workings of his brother's mind had interested him even less than LBC, and that had left him clueless when thrust into this new role. Xavier had helped Val through some sticky mining contracts, and Val had sat in on the interview with Laurel, but then they'd drifted back into their respective corners. Their relationship didn't feel any more cohesive. Maybe by design.

They'd never been close. But then Xavier had never been close to anyone except his father. That betrayal would likely always be fresh enough to serve as a reminder of what happened when you trusted people enough to let them in.

"I'm fine with seeing what happens," Laurel informed him without a lot of fanfare. "I'm not much of a five-year-plan kind of girl."

That piqued his interest. "So you'd describe yourself as spontaneous?"

What was he hoping to get out of a question like *that*? Nothing remotely professional or even anything

in the realm of strategy could come out of something that sounded more like first-date small talk.
She should shut him down.

But she nodded, treating him to a smile that had
secrets laced through it. "I'm full of surprises. And
I like them, too."

That made one of them. "I'll keep that in mind.
Tell me about your fundraising experience. I never did
hear what qualified you to be my strategy partner."

Good. That was exactly what they needed to be
talking about. No more first-date type questions that
made him to want to get to know her better, as if they
had some kind of future.

"I worked in a women's shelter," she said. "The
women who came in looking for help…you can't see
them with their slumped shoulders and tired eyes
without wanting to pour everything you've got into
erasing all that defeat. I didn't have any of my own
money to give, so that meant I had to be creative in
how I ensured we never had to turn away a single
one due to lack of funds."

He blinked away the miasma of Laurel that had
fallen over him as she caught him up in her passion.
It was easy to see her point about people donating to
her cause simply because she believed in it enough
to get them to open their checkbooks. And easy to
see why he'd yet to turn a corner on his own donation task—because he had none of that passion. For
anything. Let alone LBC.

"I had to succeed," she continued somewhat
fiercely. "Failure meant there was a woman out there

who couldn't leave a bad home where she and maybe her kids were being hurt. I couldn't have that on my conscience. So I didn't fail."

"Failure is never an option." *That* part he knew all about.

Her brief smile didn't reach her eyes. "Right. That's why I wanted to help you. We'll be a formidable team because we're exactly alike, you and I."

"We're…um, what?"

"Alike. Peas in a pod." She circled an index finger between them. "You need to succeed at this fundraiser so badly that you hired someone to take over operations so you could focus on it. Because you can't fail. I get that."

She wasn't supposed to be getting ideas about anything other than a fundraiser that would fill LBC's coffers. Her canny insight crawled through him in a way he didn't particularly like, mostly because he didn't enjoy being so transparent when his goal had been to uncover *her* vulnerabilities. "I hired you to replace someone who had resigned. Reading into the subtext is not in the job description."

Laughing, she shook her head. "Lucky for you, that skill came with the rest, so you got it for free. If I'm wrong, say so. Otherwise, let's be real with each other. That's the only way for a partnership to work."

She wasn't wrong. But that didn't mean he had to announce it. Her comment had been founded on the premise that he cared whether or not their partnership worked. Not so much. He liked depending on Xavier LeBlanc only.

"We're here."

Wisely, she didn't press him on it and chose to exit the limo. But the knowing look she shot him as he extended his arm to sweep her into the restaurant said she was still analyzing subtext and had likely concluded that he'd changed the subject on purpose.

And hell if he didn't admire a woman who could do all of that without breaking a sweat. He'd have to work extra hard to stop admiring her. Otherwise, he might end up liking Laurel Dixon, and that could not work out well when his sole goal for the evening was to seduce her into a false sense of security, then prove his suspicions about her.

Five

Laurel was in a lot of trouble.

The longer she stood at Xavier's side and covertly watched him contemplate the chocolate sculpture, the more she wanted to crawl all over him and have her wicked way. If he would unbend enough to let her. And if it wouldn't compromise everything she was trying to do with LBC.

But...

The things a tuxedo did to that man's body defied description. He wasn't just good-looking or handsome. Xavier was lip-licking, finger-smacking, eat-him-all-up *hot*. It took considerable effort to pretend she was focused on the edible art surrounding them at the gallery sponsoring the autism benefit.

Dinner had been hard enough, when she'd gotten

a solid hour just to look at him. Now he was close enough to touch and holy hell did she want to indulge her piqued curiosity.

If he tried to kiss her, she feared she wouldn't be able to stop herself from a thorough investigation of how good that could get.

As a distraction, she let the video play in her head of her greatest nightmare—the rebuttal story proving that Laurel had falsely accused the mayor's office of collusion. A rival news channel produced evidence that Laurel's sources weren't credible. That story had been all over the place the morning after she'd broken hers. Honestly, she was lucky the mayor had agreed not to press slander charges even after she publicly apologized and posted a retraction.

The shame of having made a mistake of that magnitude would never fully go away.

But ensuring she had all the facts *this* time—that was happening. Xavier was the key.

Which meant she had to stop imagining what his bottom lip would feel like between her teeth.

"I think it's supposed to be the *Venus de Milo*," Xavier commented finally and glanced at Laurel. "Do you see it?"

Yes. Art. That was a much better distraction. They were at an art show, supposedly doing field research on fundraising. "Um…yeah, I can kind of see the resemblance. If you squint and pretend that blobby thing at the top is a head."

He let his mouth curve up into a half smile. "Actually, that's what I do when I look at the real *Venus de Milo*. I skipped art appreciation in college."

She had to laugh because art wasn't really her thing, either. "I skipped everything in college in favor of working my butt off to graduate with no debt."

"That's admirable," he said as they moved to the next edible art contribution, a replica of Monet's *Water Lilies* made out of crushed hard candies.

So far, they'd seen the chocolate statue of questionable composition, a portrait of Homer Simpson formed from Rice Krispies cereal and a very good representation of a fish tank laid out in a cast iron skillet with whole sardines posed to look like they were swimming through sage seaweed.

"Life Savers," Xavier declared with certainty as he swirled his finger in the air around one of the lilies. "The candy, I mean."

"Jolly Ranchers," Laurel said just to be contrary, though what she'd hoped to get out of that, she had no idea. Xavier didn't get riled. Ever. That was one of his most maddening qualities. No matter what she did, he took it in stride, never raising his voice or really seeming to get emotional about much of anything.

She had a perverse need to find out what *would* get him riled. What he was passionate about. What might pull him out from behind his corporate facade. Or, at least, what might move him enough to throw caution to the wind and act on the sizzling chemistry between them.

Because, honestly, nothing could distract her from

wanting to know what it would be like between them. She could guess. Fantasize—and had done that a lot. But nothing satisfied her itch for knowledge. If she'd been the one in the Garden of Eden, no snake would have been required to entice Laurel into eating that apple; she'd have been climbing a tree trunk the first day.

Which was a problem.

"You think?" Xavier responded mildly, true to form.

Laurel rolled her eyes with a laugh. "Of course. Jolly Ranchers shatter when they break, like ice or glass. Life Savers crack into big chunks. See the long shards in the leaves? Definitely Jolly Ranchers."

He crossed his arms, the art completely forgotten as he contemplated her, intrigued. "Spoken like a woman with experience breaking things. Do you have a temper I should know about?"

"Maybe I get a little spirited on occasion, sure. But I only destroy candy for fun."

"I must know more about that."

She shrugged and opted for honesty. "I like to see what happens."

"To what?"

"To everything." She spread her hands wide. "Curiosity is the spice of life. What fun is it to just unwrap a Jolly Rancher and stick it in your mouth? I want to know what happens when you hit it with a hammer. When you light it on fire. When you drop it in an ant bed. How can you *not* want to know?"

"I absolutely do." His gaze dropping to her lips as if she'd been talking about an entirely different kind of knowledge, of the more carnal variety. "I want to know everything, too. Tell me."

She swallowed as the vibe between them picked up strength, humming through the heavy atmosphere. It was so electric it became increasingly apparent there would be only one way to discharge all that energy and it wasn't an art discussion.

The real question was—would they opt to act on it?

"Well, that's the thing," she said, leaning into the conversation almost automatically. Xavier had this powerful draw that made her want to be closer to him. "You can't *tell* someone what's going to happen. You have to want to jump into that void yourself. Go on a voyage of discovery because you can't stand being in the dark. What's over the horizon? Best way to find out is to sail toward it yourself."

"Curiosity," he said with a lift of his chin. "Isn't that what killed the cat?"

"Because the cat used up all nine of his lives," she informed him loftily. "I'm only on, like, number five."

He laughed, and the rich sound pebbled her skin with goose bumps. When was the last time she'd noticed the way a man laughed? But Xavier didn't laugh very often—and wasn't that a shame? She liked what it did to her, liked being the one to entice him into it.

What more could she entice him to do?

"I'm a fan of your approach to life," he said.

The compliment spread through her like she'd just gulped the first sip of hot chocolate after playing in the snow. "More where that came from."

"Really? Like what?"

He'd uncrossed his arms at some point and somehow they'd drifted to a space between two exhibits where they weren't impeding the flow of traffic. Glitzy couples strolled past them in both directions but she had a hard time concentrating on anything other than him. She'd just noticed that his eyes turned this incredible shade of deep blue when he forgot to be impersonal and let his face reveal that she'd captured his interest.

"See? Now you're getting it. You have to ask questions, dive in. That's when you find out what happens."

Her voice had dropped in deference to their close proximity and she had to admit it was also partly because she didn't want to burst the bubble that had formed around them. Being inside this circle of two did fascinating things to her insides. She didn't want to stop discovering how deep this thing went.

"What if the thing that's going to happen turns out badly?"

The undercurrents sped up as he leaned against the wall, his gaze tuned in to hers with laser sharpness. They'd moved on from talking about approaches to life to something else entirely.

"Well, you don't actually know that's going to be the result. Right? Again, part of the discovery process. Maybe it'll be very, very good. There's really only one way to answer that question."

"I'm starting to see that point," he muttered and then cursed. "This attraction between us isn't going away, is it?"

Well, that was blunt. She might be a pretty big fan of his approach to life, as well. She couldn't help the smile that spread across her face. "God, I hope not. I like the way you make me feel."

"That makes one of us."

But he punctuated that potentially deflating statement by brushing a chunk of hair from her temple with the back of his hand, lingering along her cheekbone with absolutely no apology. His touch zinged through all her empty spaces inside, filling her instantly with heat and light.

"You don't like the crazy energy of being like this with someone?" she asked somewhat breathlessly, but there was no way to help it. The man gave her lungs amnesia and they totally forgot how to function.

He was going to kiss her. She could feel the anticipation climbing. It was in the weight of his hand as he turned it against her cheek and cupped the back of her head.

"Not especially. I'm not used to a lot of crazy going on inside," he admitted and seemed as surprised that he'd said it as she was. The comment was far too personal. But then he shrugged. "You have this unique ability to pull reactions from me that I don't know what to do with."

That sounded so promising that she leaned into his hand. "This is the part where you experiment until you figure out what to do with me."

Heat stole through his gaze as his fingers caressed her hairline. "I know exactly what to do with you. It's me I'm not so sure about."

"We're partners, remember? We'll figure it out together. Step this way, sir, and prepare to be amazed at what's just behind this curtain."

He smiled, as she'd intended, but didn't immediately pull her into the kiss she was aching for.

"Sure you want to pull that curtain back? Pandora's box is a real thing, you know. Once you open it, then it's too late. You can't stuff everything back inside."

Yeah. That was a thing. Her *worst* thing.

She'd jumped off a cliff plenty of times and only realized a half step too late that she'd lost her parachute. But she hadn't splatted on the ground nearly enough times to kill her curiosity. Besides, she'd scraped herself off the sidewalk every single time and managed to limp away from the scene on her own two legs, so...

She wrapped her fingers around his lapel and drew him into her body. Slowly. The anticipation was too good to rush. He let her extend the moment before their lips met and then he took over, claiming her mouth with such ferocious need that it robbed her of her balance.

Falling into Xavier LeBlanc was, bar none, the most exhilarating experience of her life.

He consumed her from the inside out, his mouth lighting every nerve on fire. Not a little flame like the kind that sprang up when you struck a match, but the blowtorch variety. Huge, encompassing and bright, spreading so fast that it got dangerous instantly.

She wanted his hands on her. His heat. His skin. She wanted to know what he looked like when she brought him pleasure, when he came. What color his eyes would be when he peeked up at her from between her thighs.

If she got him naked, would he finally break and show her something other than absolute control? That she'd like to see. Because, so far, he was missing the abandon she'd hoped for if they got up close and personal.

What would it take to make him lose control?

Seeming to sense she needed more, he deepened the kiss. His hot tongue slicked against hers, heightening her arousal to epic proportions. The kiss took her to another dimension where she could do nothing but feel and she never wanted to return to earth.

But then his mouth lifted from hers a fraction and he murmured, "Wanna get out of here?"

Laurel crashed into reality with a sickening thud. Of course she wanted to follow him into whatever bed, limo or hot tub he had in mind to continue this, especially if it meant figuring out his magic buttons.

But she couldn't.

How could she? She wasn't Laurel Dixon, charity director and future lover of Xavier LeBlanc. She was an investigative reporter who had a bad track record of screwing up when she let herself get distracted by a source.

And that was all this man could be to her right now—a source.

She couldn't afford to have her ethics compromised in her investigation, either. If—when—she found something off in LBC's accounting, she did not want the fact that she was sleeping with the boss to shade what she did with the information.

Fine time for this realization to surface. *Before* she'd started kissing him would have been better.

Through some effort of will she'd never possessed before, she pulled free of his delicious embrace and stepped back, hoping like hell her face wasn't broadcasting how much she hated having to do so.

"Forgive me if I gave you the wrong impression," she said smoothly and tucked a lock of hair behind her ear with feigned casualness. "But that wasn't a precursor to jumping into bed. I was curious about what kissing you would feel like. My curiosity is satisfied and now we should continue our field research."

God, she sounded like a sanctimonious prig, as if she routinely kissed men for curiosity's sake and then walked away unaffected. So not true. Not only did she not recall her last kiss, she was pretty sure she'd been ruined for kissing other men ever again.

"No problem," Xavier said, his expression blank. "My mistake."

For once, Laurel was thrilled he'd maintained his cool. How crappy would that be, to finally rattle him with her backpedaling?

Her own hands were shaking from the influx of adrenaline that had nowhere to go and she'd have liked nothing more than to sweep him back into a passionate embrace. "I appreciate your graciousness."

He lifted an eyebrow. "Is that what it is? I heard a woman say she was done. There's no option B after that."

Laurel blinked. He wasn't going to remind her that he'd been the one to question whether taking this to the next level was a good idea? He'd even given her a chance to back out before he'd kissed her, which she should have taken and hadn't. But to refuse to call her on it? That was graciousness all day long and then some.

Underneath it all, Xavier was a gentleman, and dang it if that didn't just make her want him more.

Six

The next morning, Laurel swallowed her pride and tracked down Xavier in his office with the sole intent of finding out how badly she'd botched everything the night before.

It wasn't exactly bearding the lion in his den— Xavier was more of a lion statue. When he glanced up in response to her knock, his blank expression hadn't changed from last night.

Great. They were back to being at odds, then. She'd have to fix that or she'd never get the dirt she needed. Her problem was that she hadn't been prepared for how much kissing Xavier would affect her. Her plan to get him alone outside the office hadn't worked out quite like she'd hoped. If anything, they were *less* cozy than they'd been before.

"Did you need something?" he asked.

"I have to apologize for last night," she blurted out, which had not been even number ten or twelve on the list of things she'd meant to say.

What did she have to apologize for? It was her right to back off if she wanted to. The problem was that she hadn't wanted to. She genuinely liked him, which might be her biggest stumbling block at the moment.

He lifted a brow with that maddening calm. "For what?"

"Because we never really talked strategy. We got…distracted."

"That we did." He leaned back in his chair and swept a hand at the empty chairs near his desk to indicate she should pick one. "Tell me what you thought of the exhibit."

Something pinged through Laurel's chest as she absorbed that he wasn't going to punish her for backing off last night. He'd even repeated "we" as if it was partially his fault, when in reality, Laurel had been the one to push him toward a cliff he hadn't seemed terribly eager to fling himself off of. At least, not until he'd jumped and then masterfully taken control of that kiss.

Bad thing to be thinking about. His lips pursed slightly as he waited for her response, and the memory of the way that man's mouth felt on hers sliced through her again with a muscle memory that centered in her core.

Her face flushed and she scrambled into one of the

chairs, hopefully folding herself into it before he figured out how much that kiss was *still* affecting her.

"The exhibit was interesting," she began, praying her mojo would magically appear. "But I didn't like it as a fundraiser."

"Why not?"

She shrugged. "No one really wants edible art. To assume you'll sell pieces to wealthy patrons as the main means of generating donations is faulty logic."

"But the cost of admission was nothing to sneeze at." Xavier's dark blue eyes narrowed as calculations scrolled across his expression. "Surely ticket sales will bring up the total figure."

Yes, *this* was the conversation they should have had last night, but instead, she'd gotten all caught up in the vibe. "Doesn't work that way. The venue wasn't free unless the art gallery gave the autism group a block of time as a donation. Sometimes they do, but it's pretty rare, particularly if the event occurs during normal business hours. Because then the gallery is dealing with lost sales, as well, right?"

"Right. But they benefit from the publicity. So it can be a win-win situation to write off the loss."

God, the man was sexy when he was using his brain. She loved watching him think, loved how he woke up her blood with nothing more than a well-turned phrase. The best of both worlds—Xavier was smart *and* gorgeously built.

Why couldn't she have met him under different circumstances?

Shaking that off, she tapped the desk for emphasis. "There's still the cost of the buffet and bar. Again, possibly it was all donated, but that's even more unusual. Catering companies get requests for donations all the time, so they typically deny everyone in order to be fair. It's more common to pay event expenses out of donations."

"That seems counterintuitive," Xavier argued and leaned forward on the desk, folding his hands over the paperwork he'd been reviewing when she walked in. "The more money you spend, the less goes toward the cause. I don't like that at all."

She couldn't help but smile at his enthusiasm. Or what passed as such when it came to Xavier. Some people jumped around when excited. He leaned on his desk. But it was a victory nonetheless, since she had his absolute attention and she got to look at him as much as she wanted solely because they were talking.

The awkwardness from last night had completely vanished, thank God. Maybe she was finally getting it together.

"It's an age-old quandary, Xavier. That's why you hear so much about the percentage of a charity's funds that go to administrative costs versus how much is allocated to actual research or whatever. Do you want someone subpar running your charity who can't get a job anywhere else and is willing to work for a crappy salary? Or do you want someone of your caliber, with CEO experience, running it? You're not free, either."

His brows formed a line as he contemplated that. "Point taken. So our fundraiser needs to have low overhead and the probability of higher donation amounts."

"Pretty much."

She eyed him, trying to gauge how easily she could segue into the subject of fraud without tipping him off. The problem was, she didn't want to investigate that right now. The fundraiser discussion was much more fun and had fewer potential land mines.

Except that wasn't the sole reason she was here. Laurel squared her shoulders. Her career was at stake and so were the lives of the people being taken advantage of by a charity professing to be doing good.

That was the reason she was here.

"Sorry if this is stepping outside of bounds, but how do you not know all this?" she asked. "Isn't your last name the same as the woman who founded this place?"

"Yeah." It seemed as if he might clam up after that, but then he said, "It's not my world. It never was. I had to bury myself in diamonds to survive at LeBlanc. The jewelry business is not for the faint-hearted."

"But these are basic principles," she said cautiously, feeling out how to proceed when she didn't want to be treading this ground in the first place. "Basic accounting. Surely you've glanced at LBC's books in the few months you've been here."

He shrugged. "Once or twice. Accounting is boring. I have people for that, here and at my real job."

The relief that poured through her shouldn't have been so swift and sharp. It didn't prove anything. He could be lying. But she didn't think he was. And if not, then he probably didn't have any idea about the fraud going on.

Alleged fraud—or, at least, it was until she found concrete evidence.

When she did, people would go to jail. People she'd likely spoken to and smiled at in the breakroom. The charity would probably be forced to close. If LBC somehow escaped that fate, donations would likely dry up and Val would be out of a job. He'd seemed like a good person in the interview, and whatever happened to LBC would affect Xavier, too, especially if whatever she found implicated his brother.

Xavier wouldn't have too many charitable thoughts toward the messenger, either.

That put a sickening swirl in her stomach she hadn't anticipated.

Why had she thought going undercover would be a good idea again? The sooner she found what she needed, the better.

She had to get out of here before she started caring about the people more than the story.

Laurel's discussion with Xavier ended up being cut short due to an emergency in the kitchen with a small fire that one of the volunteers had accidentally started. No one was hurt and the fire department arrived well after the flames had already been extinguished.

It was still a timely reminder that playing with fire wasn't a good plan.

In the name of her ethics, she should stay away from Xavier. Except that made it hard to do either of her jobs, which put her in a terrible quandary.

Once the fire department finished checking the immediate area to be sure the danger had passed, they left. Quite a few people, Xavier included, pitched in to clean up the mess from both the fire and the subsequent traffic in the area. It was the perfect time for Laurel to steal away so she could do a little sleuthing.

Adelaide kept her desk spotless, with a square box of tissues in the right-hand corner and a lone pen holder on the left, an unusual placement unless the owner of this configuration was left-handed like the new manager. Laurel had noted that the first day.

The odds of Laurel figuring out how to break into the woman's computer were about zero, and she didn't want to do that anyway, since any evidence she found would be inadmissible in court. Maybe the filing cabinet had something of value she could use in her story.

Laurel crossed to the squat, two-drawer beige standalone cabinet and pulled open the drawer. The loud screech of metal on metal crawled down her spine. Freezing, she waited to see if her presence in a place she wasn't supposed to be had just been announced. But no one materialized at the door. She gave her heart permission to start beating again and blew out a breath.

The covert part of the job she could do without. She liked the rush of knowing that she'd be the one to expose the truth. This sneaking around grated on her nerves, though. She'd compromise her position here if she got caught.

Laurel quickly flipped through the first few folders, pausing at one labeled Performance Reviews. That might be interesting. Someone could have received a bad review and decided to take it out on the charity by screwing around with the books.

She pulled the file and thumbed through it quickly, memorizing names and their scores. Since most of LBC's workforce came in the form of volunteers, there weren't that many and the file strictly held signed copies, not the full detail that was likely in digital form.

Nothing of value. Moving on. She pulled out a second file and that's when Adelaide strolled back into her office. Laurel's pulse skyrocketed.

The woman stopped short when she noticed Laurel and pushed her glasses back farther on her face. "Oh, I wondered where you were."

Casually, Laurel dropped the folder back into the drawer as if she had every right to be rifling through the woman's files. Sometimes faking that things were cool would fool other people even when they'd started out thinking something was amiss. "Is everything straightened up in the kitchen?"

"As well as can be. Jennifer is supervising the last of it and I was in the way. What are you looking for? I'll help you find it."

Busted. Laurel didn't have much room to act like she hadn't been looking for something, so she had to scramble. "That's generous. I was trying to find out what kind of fundraisers Val had done in the past. So I can find some ideas for Xavier to use. But you don't have to help. I'm fine on my own."

The lie sat awkwardly on Laurel's conscience, especially when Addy shook her head with a small *tsk* sound and gave her a smile. "Please. It's no trouble. I owe you big-time and I haven't repaid you."

"You don't owe me anything. What are you talking about?"

Instead of answering, Adelaide crossed the room and flung her arms around Laurel. Mystified, she hugged the shorter woman in return, and when Adelaide pulled away, she had genuine tears behind her glasses.

"I do! I'm not dumb. I know you were behind Mr. LeBlanc giving me this promotion. He never would have done that unless you'd prompted him and I'm just… I love this place so much and now I'm in charge. It's like a dream come true that never would have happened without you."

For some reason, that made Laurel feel worse, probably because she'd only pushed Xavier into the idea so she could get closer to him. But she wouldn't have done so if she hadn't thought Adelaide would shine in the role. "You're a natural. He just needed help seeing the forest for the trees. He's a man, isn't he?"

Adelaide nodded and rolled her eyes. "Very much so. He's not like his brother, that's for sure. Val cares about LBC and loves the people he serves. This isn't just a job, not for any of us. I don't think Mr. Le-Blanc gets that."

"That's not true at all," Laurel corrected instantly. "Xavier and I went to a fundraiser last night to get ideas for LBC. He's more dedicated to this than you think."

What was she doing—*defending* him? And so quickly, too. But it didn't erase her absolute belief in what she'd claimed. Xavier did care.

When she'd last seen him, he'd been sweeping the floor alongside a few volunteers. She'd also spied him in the storeroom stacking boxes a few days ago. He didn't turn up his nose at any job, no matter how menial. That said a lot about his character.

Adelaide looked doubtful as she eased past Laurel to take her chair behind the desk as if they chatted like this every day and she always found Laurel with her hand in the filing cabinet.

"I'll have to take your word for it. Also, I don't think there's anything about fundraising in Marjorie's files. Maybe call Val? He's always got ideas."

The woman's devotion to her boss came through loud and clear, which boded well for her employment situation when Val returned to his normal position here at LBC and found that Laurel had passed her job to Adelaide. "I'm sure he does, but you're the manager. What would you do?"

Adelaide blinked so fast behind her glasses it was a wonder they didn't fly off. Had no one ever asked for her opinion before? The woman lived and breathed this place, which meant she had a vested interest in seeing it succeed. Her thoughts counted.

"I'd let the staff donate things they're good at making and auction them off," Adelaide said decisively, then glanced heavenward with a dramatic pause as if waiting for a burst of lightning from the ceiling that would fry her for being so forward. "I mean, everyone has a hobby. Like knitting or making patchwork quilts. There's a lot of downtime on some days, so we all bring our crafts to work and sit in the meal service area, so we get to see what other people can do. Some of the pieces are amazing."

The visual Adelaide had supplied unfurled in Laurel's head and it was easy to envision the staff showing off crocheted afghans or beaded bracelets. The auction was a surprisingly good idea. She liked it instantly. The staff would be involved and thus help spread the word, plus they could advertise the wares as one of a kind.

Though the pieces would be made with love, they would not fetch high prices at an auction with donors who were used to the finer things in life. Regardless, the premise had potential, especially if Laurel goosed it a little. "It's a fantastic idea. I'll bring it up to Xavier. I'm so glad I ran into you."

Laurel edged toward the door, since that was a good segue to get her out before her guilty conscience made an appearance. The fundraiser had been on her mind but certainly wasn't the reason she'd sneaked into Adelaide's office.

"Oh, me, too," Adelaide said so enthusiastically

that Laurel almost flinched. "You come by any time. I'm thrilled to have a confidante who listens to me. You're the best thing that's happened to LBC in a long time."

A *confidante*? Laurel's investigative journalist's ears perked up. "That's a huge compliment. Thank you. I am trying to help Xavier keep the wheels on. Speaking of which, would you mind if I stopped by, maybe tomorrow, to talk about some other areas for improvement?"

"Please do. My door is always open."

Laurel nodded at Adelaide, letting the other woman's infectious smile reflect in her own. The sweet lady would be a great partner in all things LBC. Much better than Xavier, whom she wouldn't have been able to stop undressing with her eyes even if someone offered her a million dollars.

Case in point: if she'd had half a brain, she could have found a friend in Adelaide much sooner, but no. She'd been too busy cozying up to the boss and letting herself get distracted.

"There you are."

Xavier's smooth, rich voice cut into her from behind and she whirled, only to get caught up in his deep gaze. He was so much closer than she'd anticipated and he reeked of masculinity, his biceps flaring out from beneath his T-shirt sleeves. She'd just seen him in his office a little while ago, but he'd been behind his desk. Now, there was nothing between them but raw need.

She breathed him in, losing herself in his potent

presence as she unexpectedly relived that kiss from last night. She shouldn't be. She should…go somewhere. Or do something. What had she been about to do?

"Was I missing?" she asked and thankfully her voice didn't crack.

What was wrong with her? Why couldn't she remember that she wasn't supposed to be attracted to him?

Maybe because she'd worked so hard earlier to ease the tension, and here they were. No longer at odds.

She'd failed to consider the ramifications of being on the same side.

"I didn't see you after the fire," he said, his voice low, drawing her into his sphere where the rest of LBC didn't exist.

He'd noticed she'd ducked out? That was bad—how was she supposed to be covert if he had his eye on her?

And yet it pleased her enormously that her absence had been noted. "I was working on a fundraiser idea."

The lie flowed from her tongue far too easily. She didn't want to be good at lying to him.

"Tell me." Xavier crossed his arms and leaned against the wall, so casually sexy that her mouth went dry.

"It's Addy's idea actually. An auction."

His beautiful lips pursed. "Like where you put bachelors up on the block and little old ladies pay ten thousand dollars to have a hunky guy show up to bring them tea all afternoon?"

"Um, not exactly. But now that you mention it, that sounds intriguing." Her gaze slid down the length of his long, lean body almost automatically, and it was such a visual treat, she did it again, but this time more deliberately. "Would you volunteer?"

"Depends." One of his eyebrows quirked as he sized her up in kind, a decidedly wicked gleam climbing into his gaze. "Would you bid?"

Oh, man. This was not one of those times when honesty was in her best interests. The acrid scent of burned sheetrock and plastic still hung in the air, a pungent reminder of how easily a flame got out of control.

"Only on you."

Dang it.

That had slipped out. But it was the absolute truth, which seemed like her default around him, and it was dangerous times twelve. She couldn't keep letting herself get sucked into him, but what was she supposed to do about how he affected her—quit?

His long, slow smile spiked through her core. The vibe crackled between them, growing with intensity as the moment stretched out. It was so delicious that she forgot why she should cut it off.

She was *never* like this with men, so forward and flirty, mostly because she couldn't trust herself not to screw it up.

But with Xavier—she could be anyone she wanted. He didn't know she had the tendency to be awkward around men. With him, Laurel Dixon equaled sexy and fun.

"I thought I'd already satisfied your curiosity. Did you come up with more questions that you have a burning desire for me to answer?" he asked, and the carnal thread running through his voice deepened.

Well, that was a leading question if she'd ever heard one.

"Maybe." God, she needed to reel it back, not vamp it up. This could not end well, but it felt as impossible to stop as it did to stuff a bullet back into the chamber once a gun fired. "The first one is—how good are you at making tea?"

He laughed, as she'd intended, and jerked his chin. "Sounds like you need to be the highest bidder in order to find out."

There were so many provocative things she could say in return and none of them were work appropriate. She *had* to back away from that cliff, the one she longed to fling herself from in order to soar right into his arms. This was just a conversation in the hallway about a fundraiser, nothing more. He wasn't serious; in reality, he'd done nothing but honor the fact that she'd been the one to cool things off last night. If she was smart, she'd keep things light, expectation free and, most important of all, impersonal.

"That's supposing that we're doing a bachelor auction when, in fact, we're not," she informed him, more disappointed than she had a right to be. "We would run out of bachelors too quickly."

"That's a shame." His blue eyes blazed with something she couldn't help but think might be disappointment. "I was really warming up to the idea."

She blinked. She had *no* business leading him on. None. It was unfair to him.

As much as she might want to pretend they were just having a conversation in the hall, there was entirely too much sizzling beneath the surface for that to be the case. Ignoring it wasn't helping and playing into it *really* wasn't helping.

She couldn't kiss him again or do anything else to act on the attraction swirling between them. If she'd been nothing more than a woman working at a charity, then all bets would have been off. Of course, if she had just been a woman working at a charity, she'd probably never have had the guts to speak to Xavier.

And she would have never willingly lied to a man she was interested in.

The entire thing made her sick to her stomach, but it was too late to backtrack now. And it was reprehensible to keep flirting with him when she hadn't told him the truth. She couldn't do that to someone she'd come to like more than she should.

"If you're on board with the idea of an auction, great," she said hoarsely, her throat tight with the realization that she couldn't have her cake and eat it, too. "You can help by talking to your friends and business associates about donating items. Instead of bachelors, the theme is One of a Kind. The more expensive, exclusive and special the items you talk them into donating, the better. Your crowd will love

the idea of bidding on things they can't get anywhere else."

He nodded, seemingly unaware of the shift that
had just occurred. Good. The less she had to talk
about it, the better.

"I can do that. It's a good idea."

That small bit of praise meant more than just
about anything else he'd said thus far. It might already be too late to avoid hurt feelings in this
scenario—she just hadn't grasped that they'd be *hers*.

"Fantastic," she said as brightly as she could and
started edging away before she lost her mind. "I'll
get started on it, then."

She fled in the direction of her small office and
thankfully he didn't follow her.

Seven

Xavier gave Laurel breathing room, deliberately not seeking her out for several days. He'd come on too strong in the hallway after the fire. Obviously. She'd been flirty and fun for a few brief moments and then it was like he'd slammed headfirst into a brick wall.

Bam! She'd withdrawn, just like at the art gallery. It was maddening, but he'd finally figured out that the problem was his. Not hers.

He was screwing up the plan. Somehow. Thus far, he'd failed miserably at figuring out what she was hiding, and instead had discovered a woman he wanted to spend time with. A lot of time, and not just in bed. That was tripping him up.

So maybe the breathing room was for him, too.

He distracted himself by digging through business contacts and buddies from college to hit up for donations. The conversations came out stilted and too formal, so it wasn't surprising that the first few calls netted him exactly zero enthusiasm from the other end of the line. It was disastrous for more reasons than one, not the least of which was the looming deadline to earn his inheritance.

He could hear his father laughing from beyond the grave. It echoed in Xavier's mind, solidifying his grim determination to succeed. Edward LeBlanc could not be allowed to win at this chess game he'd posthumously organized, though it was easy to see that his father had set Xavier up to fail, for God knew what reason.

Xavier tried again with the next contact, but couldn't get his feet under him until all of sudden, in the middle of a sentence, Laurel's voice crowded into his head.

People don't give to fundraisers. They give to causes they believe in.

He wasn't selling anyone on the auction donations because he didn't believe in LBC's mission.

That was an unsettling realization. He didn't think of himself as a selfish person or one immune to the plight of those down on their luck. Hadn't he just helped restock the kitchen yesterday, carrying heavy bags of potatoes so Jennifer, the manager of that area, didn't have to?

Charity was in his blood. His mother had founded this place, pouring her time and effort into it. Honestly, he'd thought she'd done so out of boredom.

Her husband had worked ninety hours a week; she'd needed something to do and had created a purpose for herself at the same time.

Then Val had followed her, taking up the cause when she'd retired. His brother had passion to spare, which Xavier had long dismissed as a personality flaw. Right at this moment, he might be close to admitting that his brother's inability to keep his heart off his sleeve was the reason Val ran LBC so well.

Xavier didn't have passion. He had interests. Things he enjoyed. Principles he lived by.

That obviously wasn't going to cut it here. If he wanted his five hundred million dollars, he had to be better than this, better than Val. He had to be like...Laurel.

She had passion. It had spilled over when she talked about her work at the women's shelter. Actually, she dripped conviction no matter the subject: Jolly Ranchers, the auction, Adelaide taking over management. Even her one-kiss-and-done speech had been firm, with no room for argument—the difference there being that he had a vested interest in changing her mind.

He pushed back from his desk and went in search of Ms. Dixon.

Her office was on the other side of the building, the only one that had been available once she'd given Marjorie's office to Adelaide. But she wasn't inside and her chair had been pushed up under the desk like she'd planned to be gone awhile, as opposed to having run to get coffee or something. Stymied, he scouted around for her and finally found her in one of the conference rooms.

She stood at the head of the long table talking to four extremely rapt audience members—volunteers from Northwestern University by the look of them. They were all young and wore expensive clothes that were deceptively casual. The university supplied a large number of LBC's volunteers, but this was the first time he'd realized that Laurel chipped in to help with their orientation.

Instead of interrupting her, he crossed his arms and leaned against the doorjamb to listen. And look. He wasn't blind; her sable hair hung down around her shoulders, so vibrant it was almost a living thing. He'd love nothing more than to be given an invitation to put his hands in her hair. Even brush it, something he'd never done in his life to a woman. But her hair begged to be explored.

Who could blame the newbie volunteers for hanging on her every word? The woman was gorgeous, articulate and so animated that his attention never wavered.

"So that's what we do here," she concluded. "Give people hope. The moment you start thinking that LBC is about food, that's when you lose sight of the person behind the mouth. Sure, food is important. Critical. But so is understanding what it represents. And for many of the guests, it's hope."

The four volunteers applauded and Xavier very nearly followed suit. But then she glanced up to see him standing there. A smile spread across her face that wiped all functional thought from his brain.

"A rare treat for you all today," she said and lifted a hand to indicate Xavier. "Mr. LeBlanc himself has come by to say hi."

The volunteers swiveled to take his measure, one immediately launching to his feet to cross the room and shake his hand enthusiastically. "I'm Liam Perry, sir. My father runs Metro Bank and has long been a customer of LeBlanc Jewelers. It's an honor to meet you."

"Simon Perry is your father?" Xavier asked needlessly, because of course he was. There was only one head of Metro Bank with the last name of Perry.

The kid nodded as if it was a perfectly reasonable question. "Yes, sir."

It was just that Xavier had always considered Simon Perry a peer and contemporary. Maybe not precisely the same age as Xavier, but close. And yet, the man had a college-aged son and probably other kids, too. A wife, most likely.

The concept of a family scared the mess out of him. Val's wife was pregnant and even that seemed like it had happened too soon, too fast. His brother seemed okay with it, but Xavier had never felt *ready* for something like that. And meeting Simon Perry's adult son brought it home in a different way. How did you get to a point where it didn't feel like you were signing up to get it wrong for the next two decades?

Parenting was a recipe for failure all day long. All at once, he wondered if Laurel worried about being a failure as a parent like he did. Even if she did, that did not make them alike, as she'd tried to insist was the case at the art gallery the other night.

Xavier shook off the weird revelations and made small talk with the Perry boy and the other volunteers for a minute. Then he hung out near the table while Laurel sent her charges off to Jennifer in the kitchen, where they'd be spending the afternoon prepping the evening meal.

Once they were finally alone, she contemplated him. "To what do I owe the pleasure?"

"I can't attend the orientation of new volunteers in my own charity if I want to?" Up close, she smelled like vanilla and citrus, which he would not have said went together. On her it became a magical blend that was downright erotic. "Speaking of which, when did you become the go-to for that?"

She lifted one shoulder. "I do whatever needs to be done. Marcy normally does orientations but she's taking her daughter to have her wisdom teeth extracted. So I volunteered."

These felt like things Xavier should know. It was Adelaide's job to manage the day-to-day operations, but he'd bet money Val knew who did orientations on a regular basis, plus the name of the woman's daughter. His brother would have already ordered flowers to be sent to the girl and no one would have ever introduced Val to volunteers as Mr. LeBlanc.

Yet that was the only part of this whole scenario that had felt natural to Xavier. Everyone called him Mr. LeBlanc. Xavier was too personal. Plus his name had a faintly exotic quality better suited to someone who frequented hookah lounges in Turkey and back-packed the Himalayas. Someone adventurous and irresponsible. Not the head of a near-billion-dollar corporation.

He wasn't dealing diamonds today, though. And he needed a shot of something to get him out of his fundraising slump—Laurel. How she'd become the answer, he didn't know, but he did trust his gut and it was screaming at him to embrace the idea of part-nering with her.

Going it alone hadn't worked. Time for Plan B.

"Where did you get that speech?" He jerked his head toward the front of the room where she'd been standing when she told the volunteers not to forget the people behind the mouth. "Is that part of the orientation package and you were just reading it?"

"No. It's mine," she admitted freely with a sunny smile. "I just made it up. Because it makes sense. The volunteers don't necessarily want to be here in the first place, so I try to help them see what we do is more than slapping some food into a person's hand."

Slightly agape, he stared at her. "The volunteers don't want to be here? That's a new one on me. Isn't that the very definition of the term *volunteer*?"

"You would think. But a lot of times, they're ful-filling some type of requirement to get their degree or to earn a badge. Their place of employment en-courages it, maybe. There are all sorts of reasons they end up here, and rarely is it because they have

a burning desire to hang out with a bunch of homeless people."

All of this was so foreign, as if Laurel had started
speaking in tongues. How had he never discovered
this fact or thought to ask questions about the people
who did the work at LBC? He'd been pretty focused
on fundraising because that had been the stipulation
in the will, but Laurel had just uncovered a whole
new dimension to running this place that he'd left
previously unexplored.

Probably his lack of engagement explained his
lack of conviction about LBC's mission. If only he'd
fully listened to Laurel's point about that from the
beginning.

But he was here now. Listening. Absorbing.

"You're here hanging out with homeless people
on purpose."

"I'm not a volunteer," she reminded him. "I choose
to work here because it means something to me."

That was the line he needed to press. Deliberately,
he shut the door to the conference room and leaned
on it. Interruptions of any sort could wait. "What
does it mean? Tell me why you believe in LBC."

"So you can write it down and repeat it?" She
arched a brow that said she had his number and it
was zero. "Tell me why *you* believe in LBC. What
makes you walk through the doors every day?"

Money.

The word sprang to his lips but he couldn't spit
it out. It was a cold, hard truth that money made the
world go 'round. But he had money and Laurel ask-

ing the question forced him to reevaluate. What he wanted was his *due*. What he'd already thought he'd earned by running LeBlanc Jewelers the way he'd hoped would earn his father's approval.

Instead, upon his mentor's death, Xavier had been handed a task that was nearly impossible because he lacked the fire needed to complete it. And the woman he'd hired to be his ace in the hole wasn't biting. She wanted *him* to figure it out.

So he would.

"I walk through the doors because I need to prove that I have what it takes," he told her with biting honesty. "I've been successful at everything I've tried, until now, and I cannot let this defeat me."

Her soft smile caught him sideways and he let it pour through him until he was filled to the brim.

"Exactly," she whispered. "Now imagine you're on the other side of the counter and think about what you just said from the perspective of someone who needs LBC's help."

Transfixed by her voice, he shut his eyes and did as she asked, letting the sheer helplessness of being unable to complete this fundraising task rush through him. He was no longer a CEO with all the privileges, headaches and responsibilities that came along with the role, or even a son whose father had forced him to confront his own weaknesses. He was a man who knew what it felt like to have odds stacked against him, to have no one to depend on but himself and no hope.

Laurel's soft touch nearly unglued him but he

didn't open his eyes as she slid her hand into his and squeezed.

"It's okay that you're hungry and broken," she murmured, speaking to him as if he were one of the homeless masses. "I'm here. You don't have to figure this out all by yourself. Let me feed you. Then you'll have the strength to figure out where to go from here."

Yes. He held on to her hand like a lifeline, absorbing the truth she'd so eloquently revealed. He didn't have to do this alone. Neither did the hungry people of Chicago. LBC cared enough to see the real need—and it wasn't food. It was the recovery of an individual's soul when all seemed lost. It was renewed belief in yourself.

He could sell that. Dear God, could he sell that.

His lids flew up and the look radiating from Laurel's silvery-gray eyes walloped him in places he didn't know existed. Did she fully get that she'd been talking him through his own demons as much as she'd been describing the plight of the people LBC served?

And did he really want to ask? The answer might open up dimensions to their relationship that he wasn't ready for. Neither did he care overly much for the idea of being knocked flat again if he tried to take things up a notch.

"Where did all of that come from?" he asked, his voice tight with emotion he couldn't control. "You've been here for five minutes. I've had a peripheral view of LBC for years and couldn't have articulated that so clearly."

"It came from here." She tapped her heart using her free hand without breaking their connection. "Because it's my story, too. I refuse to be defeated, but determination alone doesn't cut it."

Yesterday he would have argued with her, but today… "I'm starting to see that point."

Neither could he deny that she might have been spouting God's truth about how similar the two of them were. How else could she have verbalized the contents of his soul so easily?

"You know what hell is to me?" she asked him. "Having no one to count on. No one to support me when I've been kicked to the curb. Finding that helping hand is what gives me the strength to take the next step."

Okay, that part wasn't the same. But maybe it should be. That was the gist of this whole discussion. Determination was only the first step, and you could be determined all day long not to starve, but to prevent that, you had to take the hand of the person offering assistance.

Or in his case, he couldn't let go of the person already holding his hand.

Suddenly it all seemed so clear. Laurel had been standoffish because she knew he had issues with trust. She could read him like a book, had proven that just now. How hard would it have been for her to pick up on the fact that he hadn't been totally up front about his interest?

God, he was a moron. Of course she sensed his reticence and it had fueled her own. That's probably what had tripped his suspicions in the first place. The woman had been nothing but an asset from day one and he'd bumbled around, ignoring the partnership she'd offered. The same one she'd *told him* he needed, and he'd blown it off like she couldn't possibly join him on his island of one.

His father had done a bigger number on him than he'd realized. He couldn't fully trust Laurel to work on his fundraiser, couldn't trust her enough to be all-in with his attraction to her, couldn't trust his gut.

But he could trust the sizzling chemistry between them. That had always felt exactly right.

So he reeled her in, slowly, giving her plenty of time to clue in to his intent in case she still wasn't on board with what he'd come to realize was inevitable between them. Her eyes flared as she got caught up in his gaze. Heat climbed between them, searing the air.

"Xavier," she murmured. "We can't."

"We can," he assured her but stopped just short of sweeping her deep into his embrace in deference to her protest, opting to brush the back of his hand down her cheekbone, instead. "Not here. But soon."

She shook her head, her cheek grazing his knuckles repeatedly, but she didn't pull away. "Then *I* can't. It's—"

"Shh. I get it. You're worried about the fact that we work together." Her skin felt like poetry and he wished he had the words to describe the way touching it made him feel. "Don't be. I'm only here for a blip and then Val will be back. Until then, we're going to do this fundraising task together. It only makes sense that we'll eventually give in to this *thing* we both feel. Why wait?"

"Because *I'm* not going to give in," she countered fiercely. "You're riding high on emotions, not logic. You've let yourself be swept up in the moment."

"Exactly!" Finally, everything had clicked into focus for him and this was the moment she picked to be obtuse? It actually made him laugh. "I've never been swept up by emotions. Never. This is a first for me. Don't kill it. Help me embrace it."

"Xavier—"

"No, Laurel, don't. I need you. Let me be passionate about this. Let me romance you while we're working on the fundraiser. I'm probably going to suck at all of the above, so you'll have to tell me when I'm screwing up." He smiled, pulling one from her, too. "What breathing woman would turn *that* down?"

Somehow, she managed to laugh and shoot him a dubious smirk at the same time. "If you'd let me get a word in edgewise, I—"

"Will say yes." He nodded once and tipped her head up to brush a thumb across her bottom lip. She didn't pull away, and in fact, leaned into his touch with a smile. It was enough.

Flying high on that small bit of acquiescence, he fused their mouths together, drawing her into an instantly deep kiss. Her squeak of protest died when she eagerly met his tongue in a hot clash of need. Her arms clamped around him, fingers sliding along the back of his neck as she held on, urging him forward.

He took the prompt and hefted her more solidly into his arms, reveling in the feel of her body snug against his. Yes, that was the theme of this kiss. *Feel.* He wanted to feel her skin, her hair, her hands racing down his body, but he settled for this fully clothed kiss in the conference room of LBC.

There was plenty to experience. Laurel tasted like the best combination of sweetness and heat as she kissed him. Apparently, he hadn't situated her properly enough for her liking because she burrowed deeper into his arms, her hips aligning with his so perfectly that it knocked all the air from his lungs. God, she was something. A live wire that electrified his whole body. If he didn't stop now, he feared his hair would end up singed.

He didn't stop. He tilted her head to find a new angle and it was so much better that he couldn't help letting his hands wander to her amazing backside. It was firm in his palms, promising that she would be spectacular naked. Not that he'd ever thought otherwise. But with that small preview, his need for her shot into the red.

"Laurel," he muttered huskily as he pulled back to rain nibbley kisses along her jaw. "Dinner. Me and you. Tomorrow night."

Her answering breathy sigh sounded like a yes to him. He nibbled on her earlobe, gratified to feel her sharp intake of breath as her chest expanded against his.

"Xavier, I—" She gasped as he sampled the skin below her ear, sucking on it probably a little too hard to leave it unmarked, but oh, well.

He liked the idea of Laurel wearing his lip marks. But it sounded even better to hide them beneath her clothing. It would be a secret that only the two of them knew. Carefully, he drew her blouse off one shoulder, following the line of her collarbone with open-mouthed kisses. Her body swayed toward him and he steadied her with one hand to the small of her back.

That creamy expanse of shoulder that he'd been dreaming about since the art gallery beckoned, and he abraded it with his mouth. Her hands came up to grip his T-shirt and then twisted, yanking him closer as more of those breathy sighs ruffled through his hair.

When he lifted his mouth, the red mark wasn't any bigger than a dime, but it gave him an enormous sense of satisfaction just the same. "After dinner, I want to put more of these marks on you. On your thighs. At the small of your back. The curve of your breast."

Her eyelids fluttered closed in an apparent quest for fortification. He hoped she didn't find it because he wanted her defenses down. He wanted her open and affected, wearing nothing but her enthusiasm for life.

"You can't say things like that," she whispered.

"Because it's inappropriate?"

"Because it makes me want that!" She blew out

a frustrated breath. "This is all wrong. I'm not supposed to want you this much."

He couldn't help but grin. "I'm really not seeing the problem, then. Just let me take you to dinner. No pressure. I need a plus one. For a thing at Val's house. Very casual, other people there. No chance I'll drag you into a back bedroom and ravish you."

Or rather, there was a 100 percent chance he'd do exactly that if she gave him the slightest sign it was something she'd welcome, but she didn't have to know that. For some reason, she was holding back, probably because she still thought she sensed his hesitation. He couldn't let her think he continued to have suspicions about her when he was trying so hard to be different.

"Come on, Laurel," he pleaded, letting his expression convey what was going on in his head. "Just say yes. I promise I will keep my hands off you if that's what you want. We can just spend time together. I would enjoy that. If you would, too, I'll pick you up tomorrow night at seven."

"I should say no." But she shook her head with a laugh that didn't sound at all like a no. "You promise it's just dinner and nothing more?"

"Cross my heart." Xavier pressed his sudden advantage by dropping a quick kiss on her upturned cheek and then releasing her. "See? I can stop touching you if you tell me to."

She stepped back, her face flushed as she resituated her blouse. "I shouldn't go. But okay."

That was such a hard-won yes that he broke into a

huge grin. There was no reason not to let her see how happy she'd just made him, so he didn't temper it.

He had thirty-six hours to figure out how to break down the remainder of her objections. Thirty-six hours to learn everything he could about how to romance a woman after he'd already been an idiot. Thirty-six hours to convince Val he'd love to host a dinner party for Xavier and his date because that was the only invitation she'd accept.

After the hurdles he'd just leaped over, all of that should be a piece of cake.

Eight

The next day, Xavier left LBC at noon to attend a seminar in uptown Chicago. The moment he walked out the door, Laurel sneaked into his office.

She had to find *something* she could use for her story. Anything. As long as it was concrete enough to submit her resignation before seven o'clock tonight. Then she could feasibly go on this date he'd tempted her into accepting. Otherwise, she *had* to cancel, as much as the thought of not spending the evening with Xavier made her eyes sting with unshed tears.

Yeah, she was a crappy, weak person who'd totally given into temptation. She should have stood her ground, refused to engage. Definitely she shouldn't have let him kiss her, but holy cow, how could she have stopped herself? The man had some kind of secret power that rendered her mute and stupid.

And she really wanted to go on the date. Like, a lot. Men like Xavier didn't ask her out. They didn't notice her at all. But he had. And it was screwing with her head.

As she ducked through the door of his office, she noted he'd left his laptop, but it was shut and would require his credentials to unlock. That was fine. She'd find something in his filing cabinet. But as she flipped through the file folders, the worst sense of déjà vu slowed her fingers.

What if he caught her in here like Addy had done when Laurel had been snooping in her office? Telling him the truth under these circumstances would kill her, especially after everything that had happened yesterday when she'd forgotten that she was undercover. When he hadn't let her tell him the truth. She'd tried!

That scene in the conference room had been 100 percent Laurel, no holds barred, baring her true self and begging for Xavier to do so in kind. And he'd responded to that with something amazing. He'd been so deep and personal she'd hardly been able to keep her wits about her.

Kissing him had been a natural segue, just like his request to extend the vibe over dinner. Totally reasonable, assuming everyone in the room had been on the up-and-up. It had taken every ounce of will in her to say no and then he'd gone and done the one thing she could agree to—promising her it was just dinner and he'd keep his hands off. It was the only stipulation that would have passed her ethics test.

Well, that or calling off the investigation.

Her hands froze as she filtered the concept through her beleaguered senses.

What if she did that? What if she said forget it and gave up her investigative journalist hat in favor of Charity Worker Laurel? She had a legit job here at LBC. No one had to know she'd started her stint under false pretenses, only that she'd continued it for all the right reasons—to help people. She'd just be doing it in a slightly different way.

Then she could date Xavier without fear. What would that be like?

The thought of throwing away her entire professional career made her heart hurt, though. She couldn't stop digging. LBC had a bad apple somewhere. If she gave up, who would expose the fraud? It was even more unethical to abandon the fight strictly so she could sleep with Xavier and avoid a guilty conscience. Her investigation had merit and at the end of the day, he was just a man.

Except he wasn't.

Xavier was special—she could feel it when he held her hand, see it in his gaze when he looked at her. He made *her* feel special, like he'd been pulled into her orbit instead of the other way around. They could have something amazing and she'd never get to experience it because she'd boxed herself into a corner.

Blinking back the moisture that insisted on gathering at the edges of her eyes, she forced herself to flick through the file folder from front to back. Nothing jumped out. Thank God.

She shut the drawer as quietly as possible and went on to the next, then the next, pretending she was being as thorough as possible when deep down, she knew *haphazard* would be a better term for this investigation technique. What was wrong with her?

Really, the best strategy would be to find solid evidence, get out and never darken the door of LBC again. If she didn't see Xavier every day, she wouldn't want him so badly. The man even smelled like erotic suggestion. His aftershave had some kind of earthy note to it that made her think of sex. Or maybe that was just because *he* was that potent and pretty much any time she came in contact with him, images of the two of them twined together sprang to mind.

Oh, who was she kidding? She thought of that even when he wasn't in the room. She'd said yes to dinner because she'd secretly hoped some magical solution would present itself that would allow everything to work out.

Xavier's office had nothing she could use, no obvious hint of fraud lying around for her to find. Bummer. She had four hours to decide whether or not to stand him up for their date or go anyway while pretending that it was "just dinner." Instead of weighing that out, she ended up using those four hours to berate herself for letting her feelings for Xavier get to this point.

Bottom line—it was already too late. Her investigation had been irrevocably compromised.

Now what? Jump into Xavier with both feet and see how everything shook out? It was entirely possible that she'd never find evidence of fraud. Then she'd have given up this chance with Xavier for nothing.

While her conscience battled it out, Laurel got dressed for a casual dinner at Val's house because she'd already agreed to it. It would be bad form to cancel at this late hour, right? She could always invoke the hands-off rule; Xavier had said it was her call.

But when she opened the door at seven, the man on her doorstep took her breath. Xavier wore the hell out of a long-sleeved Henley the same color as his eyes and dark jeans that hugged the lines of his body so nicely she could almost feel the drool forming in her mouth.

"Just to be clear," she said, "if I say you have to keep your hands to yourself, do I have to follow the same rule?"

"Absolutely not," he replied instantaneously, a wicked gleam spreading through his gaze as if she made comments of that nature all the time and he liked it. "You don't have any rules. Not one. You feel free to touch me whenever and however you want."

"Noted. So, I guess we should stop all the make-believe and admit that this is not just dinner."

This was Xavier's inherent danger. She had no filter around him, because he made her brave. Every time he got within two feet of her, she forgot to be awkward and she could not possibly express how much she appreciated that.

"I don't know what you're talking about." Xavier spread both palms in the air in the classic hands-off gesture. "Val's having a get-together, and since he's going to be your boss at some point, it's a chance to socialize ahead of time. I was just invited because he's my brother. We'll eat and there will be some conversation. If you want to read into that solely because I'm imagining what you look like under that dress, I can't stop you."

Her smile shouldn't be so wide. In fact, she should take him to task for being so forward, but the time for that had long passed. "I've got on a matching pink panties and bra set that I bought to wear the next time I had a hot date. I figured it was time to pull it out since it's been sitting in the bag for something like six months."

The heated gleam in his gaze went thermonuclear. "I can envision it perfectly. Shame that's all I'm going to get to do, since this is just dinner."

Somehow, his insistence on maintaining their artificial distance despite her provocative comments put her in a daring mood. It was Friday night and she could separate her personal life from work. Plus, there was no guarantee she'd ever have to worry about the results of her investigation.

Especially if she kept up the half-hearted techniques she'd used thus far. She'd really have to give herself a stern talking-to. Tomorrow.

Until there was something to worry about, there

was no reason to keep refusing to explore what might be a really good thing with Xavier. Was it so bad to ignore the complications for a few hours?

She made an iron-clad deal with herself: if she did find anything, she'd bring it to him first and ask permission to report on it. If he was the kind of man she thought he was, he'd be glad she'd done so and agree to the story. She refused to believe he'd brush it under the carpet, but if he did, then she'd know he wasn't a man she could fall for, and she'd have every right to break the story without his consent. That was the best she could do under these circumstances.

As of right now, she wasn't an investigative reporter. She was Laurel Dixon, a woman with a great man on her doorstep who wanted to take her to a get-together at his brother's house.

Val lived in River Forest, which was so far from Laurel's tiny clapboard house it might as well be in Timbuktu. The gorgeous, sprawling home her future boss shared with his wife defied description. Laurel drank in the enormous trees and manicured lawns as Xavier wheeled his slick sports car up the drive.

So much for pretending this was a normal date with a nice guy she'd met at work. Of course, that had pretty much flown out the window the moment she slid into the buttery leather seat of the Aston Martin Xavier drove that probably cost double the amount of her college education.

"I'm guessing your house could give this one a

run for its money," she commented wryly as the car slowed to a stop by the massive double front door.

Xavier glanced her. "I wasn't aware there was a contest. If it's age, then no, Val's house wins. It's historic. Not my thing, but he loves it."

Obtuse on purpose to steer the conversation away from the vast wealth of the LeBlanc family? Unnecessary. She knew they had a lot of money; after all, he'd picked her up for the art gallery gala in a limo—and she *could* read. Did he honestly think she'd never Googled him?

"No contest. It just occurs to me that I'm not in Kansas anymore."

"Does the money bother you?" he asked quietly as he switched off the car.

Silence fell inside the small, cockpit-like interior as she contemplated his face, made so much more intriguing by the landscape lighting that had thrown it into half shadows. "I just forget about it on occasion. At work, you wear casual clothes and it's hard to think of you as anything other than the guy I saw with a broom in his hand after a fire."

"That's the nicest thing anyone's ever said to me."

She rolled her eyes. "I'm being serious."

"So am I." He reached out and tipped her chin up to lay a brief kiss on her upturned lips, then immediately released her. "I'm not going to apologize for that. But I do promise to keep my hands off for the rest of the evening."

Her lips tingled as she stared at him, wishing he

hadn't retreated so fast. "What if I don't want you to do either one?"

"Then you say the word," he murmured, his gaze catching hers in a tangle of heat and promise. "I'll give you a personal tour of my house. We'll start in the foyer, where I'll back you up against one of the marble columns as I strip you. I want to see your skin against it. Maybe next I'll introduce you to the couch in the library. It's overstuffed, so plush you'd disappear into it, and it's a shame it never sees any action since it's wide enough for two. There's a skylight and I think it's perfectly positioned to spill moonlight all over you. I'd like to kiss every place it touches."

She shuddered as that image buried itself in her core and started simmering. "Stop. You had me at *then*."

He laughed, the low rich sound tumbling through her already-stimulated erogenous zones. "I've only just gotten started. I have a big house."

"I'll keep that in mind." That might take some effort when it was all she could think about. As he'd probably intended. The next few hours would be spent in extreme anticipation and she honestly couldn't remember a time when she'd been more enthralled by a man. "I didn't realize you were so poetic."

"I'm not." He contemplated her for a moment. "I'm only dictating what I see in my head when I think about you."

Geez. They hadn't even gotten to the really real date part of the evening and already he'd given her plenty of reasons to ditch the get-together. "How am I supposed to go hang out with actual people and make intelligent conversation when you say things like that to me?"

"The same way I've been functioning at LBC when I know you're across the building in an office where hardly anyone seeks you out," he told her flatly. "I have to stop myself at least once an hour from paying you a visit to see if your door would be strong enough to take what I've been thinking of doing to you up against it."

Well, then. Seemed like she'd given him the green light to share all his secret fantasies and she couldn't find a thing wrong with that. If this was how it was going to be between them now that she'd decided to treat this like a normal date, she was a fan.

"Maybe next time, don't stop yourself."

His gaze sharpened with hunger that thrilled through her. "I do believe you've officially blown my chances of concentrating at work on Monday."

She laughed, trying to decide if she should let herself be so charmed by him. "It's only fair. You blew my chances of concentrating at this shindig. I'm already thinking of a few excuses that can get us out of here early."

"I like the sound of that," he growled. "Maybe you can think of one that I can text to Val right now, and then we don't even have to go inside."

"That's…" She lost her train of thought as Xavier's hand settled into the hollow between her neck and shoulder, and his thumb brushed across her ear. "Um—we should at least make an appearance. They probably already know we're here."

He didn't release her. "Probably."

"We should go inside."

"We should."

And then he settled his mouth on hers in a long kiss that was clearly designed to untether her from her moorings, since that's what happened. She dropped into it, greedily sucking up every ounce of sensation. Their tongues clashed. The frissons of awareness and need that bloomed in her center sizzled along every nerve ending, and it was easily the most encompassing kiss she'd ever experienced in her life.

He palmed her jaw, one of his magic hands on each side, and angled her head to take her impossibly deeper still, as if he couldn't get enough. Good. She didn't want him to get enough. If he was never sated, he wouldn't stop. That *worked* for her.

He worked for her. He had something wholly unique that smoldered below the surface, something amazing and intense and profound. It called to her and she couldn't help but answer.

Far too soon, he backed off, his torso heaving with the effort. Or maybe that was hers. Hard to tell. There was a lot of touching and an inability to speak going on in Xavier's car.

"We should—" He nuzzled her ear and rained little butterfly kisses along her cheek. "Um…go—somewhere."

"Uh-huh." She tilted her head to give his questing mouth better access to her throat. "Like your house?"

He groaned, his lips vibrating against her skin. "I

wish you hadn't said that. Because you really sold me on your point that we had to make an appearance. It would be crappy to just not go in. Right?"

"I guess. Maybe we can think of it as foreplay."

"Or we can have a prearranged signal. You caw like a bird and I'll meet you in the bathroom," he suggested hopefully.

"Gee, that's romantic for our first time." She elbowed him playfully and then laughed when he nipped at her shoulder. "Keep thinking."

"I'm thinking I have to get out of this car before I do something irreversible," he grumbled. "I never would have pegged you for a romantic."

Because she wasn't, and it pleased her enormously that he'd clued in to that, especially since she'd been totally kidding. But she didn't correct him. What would he come up with instead, now that she'd challenged him? She burned to find out.

Somehow they made it out of the car with all their clothing intact. Xavier held her hand as they stumbled up the front steps, whispering and giggling over secret jokes that had just become a thing between them. It thrilled her. Look what she would have missed out on if she'd stuck to her ethical guns. It would have been practically criminal to give up this breathless sense of anticipation and the grin she could not wipe off her face.

A uniformed woman with steel-gray hair ushered them inside the grand foyer and Laurel pulled her attention from the perfect curve of Xavier's earlobe so she could properly greet her soon-to-be boss if her investigation stretched out much further. Val introduced her to his wife, Sabrina, who had eyes for no one but her husband. It was sweet the way she shot him little loving looks when she thought no one was paying attention.

Laurel paid attention. Apparently, her investigative brain hadn't been completely saturated with Xavier. Somehow, there was enough heightened awareness flowing through her senses that she easily picked up on the vibes in the room. Val and Sabrina were clearly very much in love, and she had a glow about her that could create some extreme envy.

The uniformed woman passed out stemmed glasses of chardonnay but gave Val's wife a glass of deep red liquid—cranberry juice if Laurel didn't miss her guess. Laurel lifted her glass as Val made a lighthearted toast to crisp fall Friday nights. That was the kind of small moment she liked to celebrate, too. She and Val were going to get along famously.

If her investigation dragged out that long.

The thought set her back. She couldn't seem to stop wondering what it would be like if this was her real life. If she kept her job at LBC, where she could still make a difference, and kept dating Xavier until— Well, that was putting the cart before the horse.

Until what? They hadn't even slept together yet. Maybe he'd be a dud in bed.

That nearly sent her into a round of uncontrollable laughter. Maybe the moon would turn into Swiss cheese, too. Her problem was that, so far, she liked being Laurel Dixon, charity worker, and she suspected that it was only going to get better.

"Sabrina's pregnant," Xavier said into her ear as Val's wife went to attend to a matter the caterer had brought to her attention while Val fiddled with the stereo system tucked into the entertainment center across the room.

"Oh?" It was such a personal thing to share. What was she supposed to do with that? "Should I congratulate her?"

"I'm not sure it's public knowledge."

She *really* didn't know what to do with the fact that Xavier didn't put her in the same category as *the public*. "Are you sure you should have told me, then?"

His brief smile tingled her toes. "I wanted to. It's kind of tripping me up."

"It is kind of a screwy thing," she said slowly, trying to parse out his intent. "Makes you think. I mean, not like, hey, I want one of those. But more about your own mortality."

His eyes flared with something she wished she could reach out and touch.

"Exactly," he murmured. "Though I don't know why I'm shocked that you read my mind. I guess we are a lot more alike than I had been willing to admit."

That's when it struck her that she'd finally gotten to the point where he was sharing his secrets with her—unsolicited. This kind of rapport couldn't be bought. It was gold for an investigative reporter. And it made her feel like crap that she was still lying to him about her identity.

There was a part of her that wanted nothing more than to stop the investigation cold. Right then and there. Make it vanish. It just didn't feel worth it in that moment.

Except, being undercover had been a convenient shield that allowed her to be much braver than she could credit herself with normally. Ever since her career had crashed and burned, her fear of failure was too ingrained to allow her to take chances with men. With that shield removed, would she shrivel up again, unable to have a conversation with a man who affected her as much as Xavier LeBlanc did?

Because that wasn't going to work at all.

She wanted to be this Laurel Dixon, the one Xavier shared things with because he trusted her, nuzzling her ear as he did it. She liked who she was with Xavier. She liked that he brought it out in her.

Was there a way to be both versions of herself without screwing it all up? Her track record didn't speak well for the possibility. But she couldn't stop walking down this path that had opened up to her in the span of a few glorious moments.

It was the worst dichotomy—she yearned to discover everything she could get her hands on, to turn over each rock and explore all the crannies, but she couldn't stop being afraid that very thing would cause her downfall.

She had no choice but to be *both* of those people.

Nine

Xavier had thought being around Sabrina again might be weird, since he'd dated her before Val had, but Laurel had taken up so much real estate beneath his skin, he forgot Val's wife was in the room the second she stopped talking.

Honestly, he'd never been all that into Sabrina in the first place and had moved on pretty easily after she'd dumped him. Sabrina was beautiful in the same way a frozen tundra dotted with snowy trees had appeal—the farther away you viewed it from, the better. That philosophy pretty well summed up how he'd always approached relationships. Maintaining distance came naturally as he worked ninety hours a week at LeBlanc Jewelers, and it also served to ensure women didn't get ideas about the longevity of their association with him.

He'd never thought twice about it, never missed a woman after she'd left, scarcely noticed if one never returned his calls.

Until Laurel.

She was so not his type. He'd have passed right by her as a potential lover if not for the fact that he'd been convinced she wasn't on the square. That suspicion had fueled their interaction from day one and he'd had a devil of a time letting it go, something he attributed to lingering bitterness over the way his father had forced him to jump through hoops.

But now he wasn't so sure. Seeing Sabrina again reminded him that he'd always kept women at arm's length, and not just because trust had become a scarce commodity in Xavier's world. He'd just never been that interested in diving deeper.

Until Laurel.

He had a feeling he'd be repeating that a lot over the course of the evening. Mostly because he wanted to do things differently, see how it felt to be fully engaged. To trust that things could only get better the more invested he became.

So…how did he do that?

After dinner was over, the couples moved to the casual living area off the kitchen. Laurel and Sabrina sat near each other on the long sofa near the fireplace, chatting up a storm. Val had set up camp near where Xavier stood by the double French doors leading to the covered patio that overlooked the pool.

They'd been talking shop, mainly about the failing New England division under the LeBlanc Jewelers umbrella that Val had been struggling to correct. But that conversation had wound down and Xavier wasn't putting a whole lot of effort into starting a new one because watching Laurel was far more fun.

Somehow, he had to figure out how to stop automatically creating distance between himself and a woman. After the scene in the car, when it seemed he'd melted the last of her objections, he'd kind of thought everything would fall into place. Now he wasn't so sure.

"So," Val said, followed by such a long pause that Xavier glanced at him expectantly. "This is a thing, then. Between you and Laurel."

"Depends on your definition of a thing."

Xavier took a long, pointed pull from his beer. With his mouth busy, he couldn't say more and he didn't intend to. Mostly because he was still trying to work through his next steps. An audience wouldn't help.

Val didn't bother taking the hint to butt out. "A thing. As in you and Laurel are dating. Which I never saw coming, by the way. I wondered why you were so hot for me to invite you over tonight. Sabrina and I canceled our previous plans, you know."

"You shouldn't have," Xavier responded mildly. "And it's not a thing. It's…"

What was it? Complicated?

It shouldn't be. Tonight they'd turned a corner of sorts, and he couldn't wait to get Laurel alone. So why was he still here, still sorting through his strategy? This part should be a snap. He'd never had trouble getting a woman into his bed.

Except this one. It was still tripping him up. *She* tripped him up, had since day one.

Sometimes when he looked at her it felt like his brain had been sucked out of his head through his ear. What was he supposed to do about that? If he couldn't think, he couldn't maintain control, let alone ensure he could see what was coming. No surprises. No blindsides.

Of course, it didn't seem to matter how alert he tried to stay around her. She still managed to pull the carpet out from under him twice an hour.

Val's eyebrows quirked. "If it's caused you to be at a loss for words, it's a thing. And that's why I canceled my plans. I had to see the lady firsthand who had prompted this round of finagling. Imagine my shock when you walked through the door with your new services manager."

"About that." Probably Xavier should have mentioned her role shift sooner, but it served multiple purposes to mention it now, not the least of which was a subject change. "Adelaide took over that position. Laurel is helping me with fundraising instead."

"It's like that, is it?" Val grinned, his dogged determination to stick with this subject apparent. "Keeping her close for some after-hours action?"

"No, it's not *like that*," Xavier countered fiercely and lowered his voice, one eye on Laurel in case she wasn't as involved in her conversation with Sabrina as he'd assumed. She didn't need any new excuses to throw up roadblocks. What would she think if she overheard their relationship being labeled something that she didn't agree with? "She's got a lot of great ideas and she's—I don't know. Inspiring. She makes me think about things a different way."

Wow. That had peeled off his tongue with literally no forethought, but it was pure truth. She was all of that and more. Five minutes ago, he'd have claimed that his sole focus with Laurel had to do with getting her into bed, but clearly there was more here than just sex. She did get him thinking in new directions when it came to his inheritance task. When it came to his approach to helming LBC as a whole. Was he supposed to feel so dazed to discover it, though?

"Yeah. That's what I meant. It's like that." In a totally unexpected move, Val socked him on the arm playfully, the way a brother who cared might. "She gets you fired up. When's the last time you raised your voice? Over anything? Laurel is obviously special. Just do me a favor and don't be yourself. I'd like to keep her at LBC."

"What the hell is that supposed to mean?" Xavier shot back and had to lower his voice again. Twice in one conversation? Laurel did have him twisted around—and they hadn't even slept together yet.

How much worse was all of this uncertainty going to get by dawn if he did get her into his bed tonight as he'd planned?

"Remember that she's a human being with feelings," Val said easily. "Women like it when you acknowledge their existence and take them out on dates occasionally."

"I'm here, aren't I?" he growled.

Which had pretty much been Val's point, as indicated by the look his brother gave him. "Yes, you are. Make the most of it. She's obviously good for you. Let her continue that trend."

Val broke off as Sabrina called to him to ask his opinion about moving to the patio. But Xavier held up a hand before his brother could answer.

"As much as we appreciate the invitation, Laurel and I will take a rain check on the rest of the evening, if you don't mind."

Hell if he couldn't take Val's hint. The reason he hadn't figured out his next steps yet had just crystalized—it was because he was supposed to do it *with Laurel*. This wasn't a solo journey. Besides, she'd been in the driver's seat since day one. Instead of wrestling back control, the key had to be letting go. It wasn't so hard to determine how this should work, after all. If he wanted to be different with a woman, he had to let the woman guide him.

Laurel met his gaze from across the room, and that otherworldly sensation rocketed through him again, like it had from the first. But this time, he recognized it as *connection*. She got him in ways he'd never wished for, never wanted.

It was too much. With nothing more than a look, she'd stripped him raw, exposing him, as if she could read the things written on his soul.

This was what he was supposed to embrace? It was madness.

Yet, he couldn't look away. She drew him into her chaos and he had zero desire to break free. Not when it felt like he was on the brink of something cataclysmic. The only thing he had to do was follow her.

Except he was the one who held the keys to their escape. It was on him to perform the extraction, so he said his goodbyes to his brother and Sabrina, then hustled Laurel into his car.

"That was the hastiest exit I've ever seen." Laurel's smile lit up the dark interior of the car as she let her fingers drift down his arm suggestively.

It was all he could do to grip the gearshift instead of sending his fingers on a quest of their own. "It was time to go. I have lots of evening left to fill and the things I have in mind can't be done at Val's house."

"I like the sound of that. Dare I hope that means you're taking me on a scenic drive along Lake Michigan?"

His mouth fell open a little wider than he'd have liked. "You're kidding, right?"

Her quick, sharp laugh loosened his lungs and had the odd effect of tightening everything else.

"I misspoke. What I meant to say was, where were we? I think your hand was under my dress, if I recall correctly," she said with a purr that vibrated through his erection, thickening it so hard and fast that he groaned.

His hand had been no such place, or they'd never

have gotten out of the car earlier. But who was he to argue? "Like this?"

He slid a palm along her bare thigh and skimmed under the hem of her dress, feathering her skin with his thumb as he went. When she didn't stop his progress, he kept going until his thumb brushed across the silk fabric between her legs. Pink, hopefully, as promised. He'd been anticipating getting a peek at the matching bra and panties set ever since she'd mentioned it earlier in the best sort of tease.

She sucked in a breath. The moment snapped with so much sexual tension that he was pretty sure his heart stopped.

"Something like that," she warbled so brokenly that he almost withdrew, but then she clamped her own palm down on his, grinding his hand deeper into her core. "But maybe more like this."

Yeah, that worked for him and then some. He circled the heel of his palm hard against her heat, yanking a gasp from Laurel that embedded itself in his nerve endings, enlivening them beyond anything he could stand. He wanted to touch her without the barrier of clothing in the way, without the center console of his car obstructing him from pulling her into his lap so he could do this properly.

"This is not the romance I promised you," he muttered. She deserved better, and he sure as hell could deliver something more fitting than a quick grope in the front seat like a randy teenager who didn't know a thing about a woman's body.

With a growl, he pulled his hand free and stabbed

the starter button, then slung the car into Reverse. "I'm taking you to my house. If you'd prefer something else, speak now or forever hold your peace."

"I'd rather hold something else. Care to guess what it is?" she asked saucily and slid her hand up his thigh in much the same fashion as he'd done to her, except she hadn't been driving at the time.

The side of Laurel's finger stroked his erection. It was the barest hint of a touch, but it felt like she'd encased his entire length in her warm palm and squeezed. The speedometer shot past ninety as the car careened up the entrance ramp to the freeway.

He forced himself to slow down before he killed someone and then he forcibly removed Laurel's hand from his lap. "Save that. We'll be there in less than five minutes."

Wisely, she chose not to press him and folded her hands into her lap. "I like your brother and his wife."

"Good," he said shortly. "I have zero interest in talking about them. If you're in a chatty mood, maybe you could list your favorite positions. Surfaces you favor. Water, yes or no? That kind of thing."

Her laugh washed over him. He glanced at her as he changed lanes to go around a minivan driving sixty-five in the fast lane, as if there weren't people behind them with a raging hard-on.

Laurel tapped her bottom lip as if contemplating. "I'm a fan of spooning. I don't like carpet but couldn't say if I did like something besides a mattress because I've never tried anything besides the two, and please clarify the water question. Would we be having sex in it or would you be pouring it over me?"

"Yes," he said instantly.

Water splashing down Laurel's body, droplets clinging to her pert breasts just begging to be licked off. Definitely that.

An image of her lounging on a stone ledge in his hot tub became superimposed over the previous fantasy. Yes to that, too. His mouth went desert dry as he imagined her spreading her legs for him in invitation, her head tipped back as she waited. The clear water would magnify her secrets, beckoning him to explore.

Why did Val have to live all the way over in River Forest? Civilized people lived in the Lincoln Park area. When he finally turned into his drive on Orchard Street and managed to get through the porte cochere opening to the garage without hitting anything, he considered it a minor miracle.

He left his car in the drive because it would take entirely too long to open the garage door. Would it be bad form to lift Laurel bodily out of her seat? Fortunately, she seemed to pick up on his urgency as her feet had already hit the pavement before he'd rounded the car to open her door. He chose to skip the admonishment. Next time, he'd get there in time to do the gentlemanly thing. Grabbing her hand, he led her to the door nearest the garage and ushered her inside.

She glanced around the darkened living area expectantly. "I seem to recall there was some talk about a marble column?"

"That's all the way in the front of the house," he said with a dismissive *tsk* and hustled her to the back staircase off the kitchen. "Way too far away. Forget I mentioned it. We'll tour the upstairs first."

They'd also skip the part where he was a moron because he hadn't had the foresight to give his staff the night off. No telling who might wander through the foyer while he was busy worshiping the goddess he'd brought home.

Once he got her into his bedroom, he shut the door and backed her against it. "This is oak. Close enough."

And then he sank into her lush mouth with a groan, molding it to his as he kissed her with every iota of pent-up longing. The awareness and anticipation that had begun simmering in the car in front of Val's house exploded into a firestorm that radiated outward to consume his entire body.

This was not the kiss he'd been envisioning. It was more. So much more. Never had he *wanted* so badly.

But he couldn't reel it back, couldn't think, couldn't do anything but feel. And she was doing plenty of that herself, her hands flat on his back, skimming downward to dip under his shirt to explore his bare skin.

The kiss deepened almost automatically as he devoured her, pressing into her delicious form until he scarcely knew where she began and he ended. Laurel's little moans of pleasure sang through him, heightening the experience even further. If he didn't hang on, he'd soar clear to the ceiling on an upward spiral of need.

Her mouth worked against his, sucking him deeper into this swirl of heat. She filled him with so many things: sensations, emotions, needs. None of which he recognized and neither could he stop the flood.

Still he didn't have *enough* of her inside him.

What was she doing to him? He never got this invested. Never got this *hot* for a woman. It was, indeed, madness in every sense of the word, as if his brain had been possessed.

He couldn't stop. He needed her skin bared, his hands on it. His mouth craved a taste of the curve of her breast, of the dew between her legs that would broadcast her desires.

As he slicked his hands down the sides of her thighs to grab the dress's hem, it occurred to him that he wasn't letting her guide him at all, and neither was he following. This was all 100 percent urgency and heat and uncontrollable desire. And yet…he struggled to find a problem with that. If they were both so overcome with eagerness, then there wouldn't be any room for weird otherworldly crap to distract him from what this was—sex. Only.

That worked for him. A beautiful woman in his bed he could handle. Why did it have to be anything else?

With a meaty growl, he picked her up in his arms and carried her to the bed. "We'll work on some other surfaces later."

She was too busy laving her tongue across his ear to do more than mumble, "That's a deal."

More gently than he'd have said his violent need would allow, he set her on the edge of the bed and leaned into her to kiss his way down her throat until he hit her dress. It was in his way. Not going to work. He yanked on the hem until it came free, then whisked the checkered print over her head.

"Holy hell." The moan that tore from his throat didn't even sound human, but who could blame him? "Pink is my new favorite color."

She smiled and fingered one of her bra straps, then drew it down her shoulder provocatively. "Maybe I'd look better out of it."

"That's not even possible." But then again... "I should probably check to make sure."

Her heated gaze latched onto his, holding it tight as he knelt between her legs to reach around her back. His fingers trembled with the effort not to rip the clasp apart. He didn't want to ruin it. But it wouldn't come apart. He cursed and gave up.

With a guttural growl, he ripped the hooks from their sewn-in prisons, the thread giving with little pops. "I'll buy you the contents of a Victoria's Secret tomorrow."

What use was money if he couldn't spend it when it really counted? He slid the bra free and forgot everything he'd ever learned—his name, how to breathe, whether he was supposed to direct the blood pumping through his heart. The perfection of Laurel's breasts called to him and he could do nothing else except answer.

Leaning forward on his knees, he lifted one beautiful globe into his palm and raised it to his mouth, sucking her nipple between his lips to taste. It was glorious. Her flesh hardened against his tongue as he licked the pointed peak.

She moaned and arched her back, pushing her breast against his mouth. He opened wider to take in more. Gasping, she clasped the back of his head, holding him in place with talon-like fingers, as if he might be interested in stopping sometime soon. Not happening. He could stay here for hours.

Except there was a whole other unexplored breast just begging for his attention. He switched sides and the second one was even more luscious than the first. Her nipple rolled between his teeth and he nipped at it, making her moan. *Again.* Harder this time. She cried out and squirmed closer, a stream of encouragement pouring from her mouth. *Yes, Xavier, like that, oh, yes…*over and over.

Emboldened, he pushed her back against the mattress, determined to build on that. Those pink panties taunted him. They covered the spot where he most wanted to be. Hooking his thumbs under the waistband, he yanked them down her thighs, then threw them somewhere. Didn't matter where. She wouldn't need them anytime soon.

"Beautiful," he murmured as he bent one of her knees so he could look his fill. There was nothing on earth more exciting than Laurel spread out on his bed, her thighs open wide in invitation. Her arousal grew more and more evident as glistening dew gathered under his watchful gaze.

Bending, he mouthed up one thigh and then settled between her legs to discover what she'd been hiding underneath that pink fabric. The first lick wound through his senses as he registered both her reaction and his all at once. Breathy sighs. Her erotic scent. Hips rolling. *Delicious*. Heat. His own gut tightening with long pulls of need.

The act of pleasuring a woman had never gotten him this worked up this fast. Sure, he liked the satisfaction of knowing he'd made a woman feel good, but this was different. Her cries inflamed him, shooting through his erection to the point where it was almost painful. He wanted *more*.

More Laurel, more feeling, more everything.

"I need you to come," he mumbled hoarsely against her sex, then increased the pressure and speed of his tongue to hurry things along. If she didn't slide over the edge in about four seconds, he'd… Well, he didn't know what he'd do, but he couldn't stand to be inside his own skin for much longer than that. He needed her more than anything he'd ever needed in his life, more than oxygen, blood, water.

And then she cried out as she clamped down on his neck with her fingers, her core pulsing against his tongue. He helped her draw it out, suckling at her pleasure bud until she sobbed his name.

The sound of her voice in the throes—it drove

him wild. He'd be hearing that in his sleep for days. Weeks. It was better than music.

Now he could take care of himself.

He shed the clothes that he'd almost forgotten he was wearing and climbed up the length of Laurel's body, kissing everything he could reach. She'd apparently recovered enough to do some exploration of her own, her hot hands stroking down his back, over his buttocks, between his legs.

She loosely gripped his erection, brushing her thumb over the tip, and hell if that didn't almost end the party in one fell swoop. The sweet sting of his arousal sharpened so fast that he had to lock it all down so he didn't come in her hand.

"Laurel." He extracted himself with a stellar force of will he hoped he would never have to replicate. "Wait."

Blindly he fumbled in the bedside table's drawer for the box of condoms he kept there and somehow got one on without tearing a huge hole in it with his trembling fingers. This was easily the most turned-on he'd ever been, and doing anything while in the midst of this much passion didn't work so well.

He settled back between Laurel's thighs. She smiled up at him, her eyes huge and full of wonderful, mystical things. Okay, *this* worked extremely well. So well that he couldn't wait a second longer. Taking her lips in a torrid kiss, he rolled her into his arms, snugging their bodies together so perfectly that it was hard to remember a time when he and Laurel weren't in this exact position.

Everything about this felt right. Exquisite. No way it could get better. And then she took him to the next level, wrapping her legs around his, opening herself up so wide that he could easily push inside with hardly any effort. So he did.

Her tight, wet heat welcomed him and she was so ready for him that he buried himself to the hilt instantly. Light pinwheeled behind his eyelids as she closed around him, squeezing him with enough pressure to pull a groan from deep in his chest.

He needed to move. She took his thrusts and then some, undulating with him until the heat and friction drove him into the heavens. He needed an anchor, something real and weighty to keep him earthbound. *Laurel*. She was the realest thing he'd ever touched, the sole tether that held him to this world.

But as he met her gaze, something inside him snapped and he soared away on wave of sensation and heat. Laurel flew right along with him, climaxing again while he was inside her, and it was everything he'd never had in a relationship before.

Everything he'd never realized making love could be.

She'd shown him the way, after all.

The fragmented pieces of this experience swirled together into one bright moment of connection and then he shattered, coming so hard that he saw stars.

He emptied himself and let her fill him back up.

When he could see again, Laurel was lying in his loose embrace, her hair mussed around her face. He couldn't think, couldn't speak. All he could do was clutch her tighter and hope like hell that she wasn't planning on going anywhere for the next month or so. He'd only just begun to explore his recently discovered passion and Laurel Dixon was it.

Ten

Laurel had to get out of this bedroom. Now. Before the huge thing inside her cracked open and let a bunch of emotions out that she shouldn't be having.

Sleeping with Xavier had been a mistake. A giant, life-altering mistake. He didn't seem too keen to let her go, though, and frankly, she wasn't sure her bones still worked. After treating her to the orgasm of the century courtesy of his talented mouth, he'd then turned around and introduced her to the orgasm of the millennium less than fifteen minutes later. The man was *amazing*.

And if she wasn't careful, she'd ruin everything.

That's what she did. Something great happened; Laurel screwed it up. It was the world's worst cause and effect. Only this time, she was in danger of losing a lot more than solely a fraud story. Her job at LBC hung in the balance, too, and she'd only just come to realize how much she valued it.

Then there was Xavier.

She didn't want to think about how quickly and easily she could mess up, especially given the flood of things happening inside. Really, she had no business being here. But how could she have refused? Especially when she'd kind of thought it was supposed to be a hookup. No fuss, everyone got some satisfaction and no one had to think about anything other than sex.

In fact, she'd tried really hard to get some car boinking going, talking dirtier to Xavier than she ever had to a man in her life. At points, she hadn't even believed the stuff coming out of her mouth.

His response? Bring her home. Like they were a couple. And he expected her to spend the night. It felt too real, too big, too much like something she'd leap tall buildings to continue.

This was not her life. Not her real life, anyway. Undercover Laurel, sure. That girl could do anything, especially since Xavier was the one who goosed her actions. That was the world's best cause and effect. Somehow, she'd find a way to mess it up, though.

The longer she lay there, spoon-style in his strong arms, the deeper the panic winnowed.

"I can feel you winding up to flee," Xavier murmured and rubbed his lips against her temple in something halfway between a kiss and a caress. "I'm not going to let you, by the way."

His mouth made her shudder. Dear God, how could the man get her so worked up with nothing more than the brush of his lips on her skin? And her temple wasn't even an erogenous zone. Or, at least, she'd never considered it one before. Right this minute, her whole body apparently fell into the category of erogenous zone as his mouth ignited something inside her.

"You can feel me thinking about leaving?" she asked, since it seemed as if her voice still worked. A minor miracle. Nothing else did, including her brain, because she couldn't remember why it was so critical that she get dressed. Only that she had to. "I didn't come prepared for a sleepover. It's better that I go."

That way she could keep pretending this was only sex.

Except he'd have to drive her or she'd have to find her phone and order a ride, which would probably take a million years on a Friday night in Lincoln Park. She was stuck for at least a little while.

"That's a complete lie," he countered and moved down to the hollow of her throat, sending her lashes fluttering as the spike of pleasure deepened. "You have all this bare skin I haven't explored yet. What more do you need for a sleepover?"

"Toothbrush," she managed to mutter. Somehow. Her skin had pebbled with goose bumps the moment he'd started talking about it.

"I have several extras. Next objection?"

"Are you just going to knock them down?"

"Pretty much. So you can save us both a lot of time by quitting while you're behind."

For some reason, his change-up of the saying made her smile. "Aren't you the one behind?"

"Why, yes, yes, I am." He punctuated that point by nestling his hips against her buttocks, announcing the fact that he'd regained a hard-on without saying a word. He pressed into the crevice with tiny, firm strokes that had her gasping instantly.

When his fingers started toying with her breasts, she nearly crawled out of her skin. How did he know all of the best ways to touch her?

"Xavier," she breathed, and it turned into a plea instead of a warning.

"Right here, sweetheart," he rumbled into her ear, and his hands slicked downward to hold her hips in place as he ground against her from behind. "This is your favorite position, right? I didn't get to it first because I'm a bad boy. Let me make it up to you."

She couldn't do anything but warble a moan in response. How was she supposed to refuse that? Answer: she couldn't. Not when his fingers crept toward her center, dipped inside and set up a slow rhythm that promised to pull her apart at the seams.

"I can't help but touch you," he continued in that slumberous voice that drifted through her very soul. "You're so sexy and warm, and I sort of lost my mind earlier."

"Ha," she said, or tried to. It came out more as a long sigh. "You've never lost anything, least of all your mind. I don't think I've even seen you get overly excited."

"You obviously have no idea what you do to me. I was nearly insane over how much I wanted you." His fingers played with her flesh as if he planned to do the same to her. Turnabout was fair play and all that. "Now that I've taken the edge off, I can do this for hours."

She didn't get a chance to revel in the victory of pushing him into something other than calm detachment. He underlined his promise with a particularly deep twist of his fingers that sang through her entire body. She bucked against his hand, instinctively seeking more. His other hand joined the party, rubbing in circles at her nub as he plunged into her core again. Pleasure knifed through her, arching her back, which allowed him to grind deeper against her buttocks.

The triple punch of sensations pushed her over the edge and she exploded in an exhilarating tsunami of passion, clenching around his fingers over and over. He did something magical, furled them in a way that elongated the orgasm, and the intensity ratcheted up exponentially.

He wrung so much pleasure out of her body that tears leaked from her eyes.

And then, after the brief crinkle of a condom wrapper, he plunged into her from behind, filling her so tightly, so fast, that it set off another round of ripples. He groaned into her ear as she kept closing around him, and that might have been the most erotic sound she'd ever heard.

Then he half rolled her to the mattress and began to move inside her, whipping her scarcely cooled center into a firestorm instantly. The heat raged as he pushed her further, demanding even more from her body, and he got it. She cried out as another intense climax seized her, and she came so hard that her legs went numb.

He followed her a few strokes later, his lips in her hair and his heavy body collapsing to cover hers as he pulsed inside her. They lay like that for an eternity until she became convinced that she'd passed into another dimension where this kind of pleasure happened to her on a regular basis.

"That was unbelievable," he croaked against her neck and rolled to settle her into his arms. "Even more so than the first time, and that's saying something."

Sweet air rushed into her lungs as his weight redistributed. She missed his body on hers instantly. Breathing was overrated. "That's one word for it."

"Give me another one," he said almost as a challenge.

"Looking for compliments?" she teased. "It was cataclysmic. Earth-shattering. Miraculous. Shall I go on?"

His lips grazed her cheek and she felt them curve upward. "You sound like a thesaurus."

Her insides froze and the silk sheet beneath her body turned cold in a flash. Of course she had a command of the English language. That's what an investigative reporter did—found the right words to describe the current situation.

The reminder was ill-timed. And yet perhaps apt. The longer she let herself stay here, the deeper she dug her own grave. After all, he still didn't know she was Undercover Laurel, and removing that barrier meant she lost all of this. Even if he didn't care, she couldn't be bold, saucy Laurel without a shield against failure.

"I feel you thinking about leaving again." His arms tightened around her, cutting off the flow of air to her lungs.

This time, it wasn't okay. She pushed at his arms until he realized what she wanted and released her, his gaze following her as she sat up.

"If you want to leave, I won't stop you," he said quietly. "I won't like it, but you do what pleases you."

That only made it worse. "Stop being so understanding."

"Okay."

"That's being understanding!"

Frustrated beyond measure, she pulled the sheet up to cover her bare breasts. Not that it mattered. He'd seen them plenty already. That was the problem, the thing she couldn't undo. They'd flung open Pandora's box, all right, and as advertised, she couldn't stuff everything back inside again.

She wanted to stay.

He didn't know the truth.

But this wasn't supposed to be serious. Any decision felt wrong, like a recipe for failure.

"You weren't 100 percent on board with coming here tonight, were you?" he asked, his voice betraying none of his thoughts. Even in this, she hadn't ruffled his feathers in the slightest.

"I was! Completely." She could own that all day long, and it was important for him to understand that she had never once felt coerced. But how did she explain the real reason she was flipping out? "I make my own choices. It's just... I don't know."

"I know," he announced, refreezing her heart.

"You do?" As in *everything*?

That wasn't possible. If he knew she'd taken the job at LBC under false pretenses, surely he wouldn't have brought her home and treated her like his own personal smorgasbord. Yet there was a part of her that craved to hear him say exactly that.

It's okay, Laurel. I love that you care enough to expose bad people in my organization. Have another orgasm or two.

"I think so. You just wanted to see how it felt to make love to me and now you're done. Just like when you kissed me at the gallery." His wry smile twisted her heart something fierce. "It's fine. My ego might be a little bruised but I'll live, as long as I did a good job satisfying your curiosity."

He was so patient, so instantly forgiving that she couldn't stand for him to think any of that. "That is so not it. I have a history of screwing up things and I refuse to do that in this situation."

Maybe that was too blunt. She'd just laid out her vulnerabilities, baring herself far more than he had when he'd stripped her clothing off. That's why she couldn't do this two-personality tango; it was too hard to juggle the woman who jumped into research with both feet and the woman who couldn't be trusted to get it right.

It wasn't her strongest play of the night, but he just nodded, taking it in stride. "You forget that we're alike. I hate failing, too, so I get that."

Oh, God, what was she supposed to do with that? Or with the little tugs at her heart that had started with his smile and had only gotten stronger with the possibility that he might actually understand her? Her vocal cords froze as she stared him, totally stricken into silence. Definitely not her finest hour.

But he didn't seem fazed at all. Gently, he took her hand, contemplating their twined fingers. "Given all of that, I've got to ask, Laurel. What do you think is going on here? If I want you to stay, am I moving too fast for you? Because that's not my intent. We're adults. I enjoy spending time with you. That's all. Don't make it into a bigger deal than it is."

She blew out a breath she hadn't realized she'd been holding. The crash and burn of her career had totally paralyzed her and it was far past time to get her head screwed on straight.

"I'm sorry. I'm being an idiot. Of course this thing between us isn't far enough along for me to be such a basket case."

Good. She could breathe. Everything was smoothing out, including her pulse.

"Basket case is going a little far," he said with a smile. "You reacted to me being an idiot, not the other way around. I don't do this kind of thing well, where I like a woman and figure out how to see more of her. Because tonight was great. Far more so than I was expecting, and selfishly, I want more of that."

"I tend to be a little cautious," she admitted. It seemed they were at a place where it was okay to confess a few things and no one had to run screaming from the room. "In the romance department. Strictly because of bad experiences."

He shook his head with a light snort. "Sweetheart, you're the least cautious woman I've ever had the pleasure of getting naked in my bed. Whatever bad experience you had that caused you to believe such a lie, banish it from your mind."

She couldn't help but smile at that, even though the only reason she'd allowed herself to get naked in his bed had everything to do with trying not to be herself tonight. Look how that had turned out. She'd nearly botched the whole thing.

"Easier said than done," she said, well aware she was treading a fine line by trying to be this person Xavier saw—the person he helped her to be. She could easily lose her balance at any moment. "I'm probably going to need lots of reminding."

"Or I can just keep you naked and let you have your wicked way with me." His naughty smirk made her laugh. "No, no. I insist. We're partners. We'll do this together or not at all."

The promise of remaining Xavier's partner thrilled her. Especially when he'd extended it to the bedroom. He was basically saying he would continue to help her be that woman he saw, the one she could only be with his influence, and that it was okay. He got it. She didn't have to be afraid of screwing up because there was nothing to screw up since they weren't serious. They were just two people who enjoyed each other and wanted to continue doing so until one or both of them ended it.

She could do that.

"You're such a trouper," she teased. "Volunteering yourself like that. How did I get so lucky as to have a partner with such a selfless streak?"

"It's nothing, really. I do run a charity, obviously because I'm the kind of guy who likes to give back." Xavier shrugged good-naturedly and tugged on her hand until she lay back down, settling her head into the hollow of his shoulder. "Now that we've settled the subject of your untimely departure, there's something bothering me about this conversation."

Since they'd just decided she shouldn't be freaking out, she tried really hard to keep her voice level when she replied, "Oh?"

"At the gallery, you talked about jumping into voids and discovering what lay over the horizon. I was pretty moved by that speech."

"You were?" She didn't recall much of anything

other than the feel of his mouth on hers. "You never said anything."

"I was trying to get a few things worked out in my head," he admitted. "I don't jump into stuff. It takes a certain kind of temperament to just blindly trust like that, and I've developed an inconvenient sense of caution lately. I'm trying to get past it. That's partially what tonight was about."

Oh, man. That spoke to her on so many levels. Emboldened, she smoothed a hand over his glorious pectoral muscle. "I'm glad I could be a part of your experimentation."

"You're not just a part of it. You inspire it."

Slowly, she absorbed that, trying to sort through what he was telling her. It sounded an awful lot like they'd just figured out yet another area they had in common. "I make you want to be bold?"

He shrugged, lifting her head a notch before letting it settle back into place. "To a degree, yeah. But I sense this hesitation in you and it's driving me nuts. I want to be all-in, Laurel, really experience what it's like to explore passion with someone. I hate this caution I've been feeling. I thought tonight would banish it, you know, if I jumped in, but then you started talking about your own caution, which doesn't jibe with the woman I've been getting to know. Maybe you're just saying that because you sense mine. I'm tripping you up."

Her eyelashes fluttered closed. Oh, God. No, that wasn't it at all. Her two-person tango was messing *him* up.

She'd never even considered that he'd pick up on all of her indecision and inability to just be herself. Of course he had. Xavier LeBlanc was not a stupid man. Yet, somehow, he'd decided that his limitations had caused hers.

"I'm sorry." What else could she say when confronted with the evidence that she'd managed to screw this up, after all?

"Don't be." He sat up, taking her with him. The covers puddled into their laps as he gripped her bare shoulders earnestly. "I'm saying I want that woman you let me glimpse at the gallery. Don't hesitate. Jump off a few cliffs in a row. I'll follow you. I want this crazy you make me feel inside. I'm sorry if the way I've held back thus far has contributed to your hesitation. Don't let it. That's all."

She stared at him, her insides a riot she could scarcely sort out. "Here's the thing. You're the one who makes me feel like I can jump. Like I can be courageous enough to put my fears behind me. Not the other way around."

A smile unfurled across his face, warming her instantly. "How about that? We're discovering how this works together. We really are a good team."

Something loosened in her chest. "I've been telling you that since day one."

Now she had to put her money where her mouth was. Xavier wanted her to be the bold, unapologetic woman she truly was inside, no fear. She had to trust that she wasn't going to mess up, trust that he was going to stick right by her side as she relearned how to be Laurel.

Because that was the best discovery of all—she wasn't two people. Just one who had forgotten how to be brave.

And brave Laurel took what she wanted.

Right now, that was Xavier.

Eleven

The weekend stretched into Monday morning and Laurel still hadn't left. That was fine by Xavier. He'd taken her shopping Saturday morning and spent an obscene amount of money ensuring she never had to leave if she didn't want to.

This was all new to him, but he liked where it was headed so far.

Especially when his alarm went off Monday morning at 5:00 a.m. and Laurel didn't stir. He'd tucked her into his embrace to fall asleep for the third night in a row, but at some point, she'd moved over to her own side, clutching her pillow like someone had tried to take it away from her. He watched her for a moment in the low light of the bedside lamp and opted not to disturb her as he went about his Monday morning routine.

Halfway through the middle of his workout, Laurel wandered into the gym. Her sable hair spilled down her back with mussed strands haloing her face, and she was easily the most beautiful woman he'd ever seen in his life. Even in sleep shorts and a tiny white tank top. Especially in that. In about four seconds, he was going to peel it off with his teeth.

"Good morning," she called with a sleepy smile. "This place is hard to find. I had to ask Greta where you were."

The immeasurable benefit of live-in staff. He rested the dumbbell in his hand on his thigh, which did nothing to free up his hands so he could pull her into his arms, but he *was* hot and sweaty. So he came up with a much better plan.

"I didn't want to wake you. But since you did that on your own, give me five minutes to finish my last set and we can take a shower together."

"Deal." She hesitated and just when he was about to remind her that he preferred it when she gave it to him no holds barred, she continued, "If you want to drop me off at home before work, that's fine."

"Why the hell would I want to do that?" He'd told her on multiple occasions that there was no expiration date to their affair and neither did he want to set one.

Sure, he was overly enthusiastic about continuing to sleep with Laurel on a regular basis. So? He had never been one to pull punches and he liked Laurel in his bed. When that changed, he'd let her know.

"Because, you know. The rest of LBC might not like it so much that I'm dating the boss."

"The rest of LBC can jump in Lake Michigan," he growled, but then had to concede that, while obviously Val knew he was seeing Laurel, the rest of the staff didn't necessarily hold the same views about dating in the workplace as Xavier did. Namely that it was none of their business.

Except he was supposed to be steering the ship until Val's return. He couldn't do what he pleased without ramifications.

It was a tricky dynamic, one he'd never had to contemplate before. What would happen when they stopped seeing each other? Would things grow uncomfortable between them or would they remain friendly, working together easily despite the fact that they no longer had the right to get each other naked behind a shut office door?

The idea of not having the right to sleep with Laurel put him in a foul mood. That was not on the horizon anytime soon, not if he had anything to say about it. Part of the problem was the fact that it wasn't all up to him. Laurel could decide at any point that she was done and there was nothing he could do to stop her.

Was it too soon to bring up the idea of something a little more permanent than whatever it was they were doing right now?

Xavier shook his head. Hard.

Yes. It was way, *way* too soon. What was he even thinking, that he'd blurt out an invitation for Laurel to move in? She'd laugh in his face and she should.

He needed to take a huge step back before he did something irreversible solely due to phenomenal sex.

"You have a point," he conceded. "The staff needs to get used to the idea that we're dating, but that doesn't mean we have to throw it in their faces. I'll drop you at your house on the way into LBC."

It was an easy solution to multiple problems. He didn't like it.

She nodded as if that had been the outcome she'd hoped for, but he couldn't muster the same enthusiasm. What if she didn't want to come back here tonight? Maybe she wanted her space. He didn't like space.

Laurel had cracked something open inside him, something that wished for more substance than a weekend affair, and now it was being threatened.

All the more reason to let her do as she pleased. He blew out a breath. Space would be good for them both. In fact, he should probably take a shower alone. This house had five bathrooms. Surely he could find one that would be Laurel free and then he didn't have to contemplate what had taken over his brain since Friday night.

"Once I have my car, I can drive myself back and forth from your house to LBC," she said with a smile. "We'll do it on the sly for a little bit until we figure out how big of a deal this is going to be for people. Maybe, eventually, we can drop the pretense and I'll just ride with you into the office. Speaking of which, if we're taking a shower, we should get started because I've been standing here aching for you to put your hands on me for a million years and the things I want you to do to me will take a very long time. We don't want to be late for work."

He got so hard so fast that he almost couldn't breathe. But that didn't stop him from picking her up and carrying her into the closest shower off the gym. As the hot water sluiced over them both, he lost himself in her soapy, sexy body.

Space was overrated.

Of course she wasn't done with him. His trust issues were rearing their ugly heads again, that was all. Until he had something to worry about, he needed to relax and enjoy the benefits of seeing a great woman who was allowing him to discover all the things he'd missed thus far in a relationship.

Despite all of that, he still had a very difficult time letting her go later that morning. Finally, she sprang from the front seat of his car, wrenching away from his kiss with the promise that she'd come by his office later.

That at least made him smile as he drove to LBC in rush hour traffic with a raging hard-on. He'd have thought the shower sex would have sated him for the morning, but no. He wanted Laurel 24/7.

She let him cool his heels for an hour. His coffee had long grown cold, but every time he picked it up, he heard a noise outside his door that he hoped was Laurel, so he set it back down again, only to be disappointed.

Getting her naked behind closed doors had become his number one priority. The amount of work he'd accomplished since arriving—zero—attested to that more than he cared to contemplate.

He should be working on plans for the next fundraiser, not moping about like a lovesick teenager. When she finally blew through the door wearing a lime-green dress that ended just above her knees, everything but her drained from his head.

"About time," he growled. "That dress is the perfect color for what I have in mind to do to you."

She shut the door and leaned against it, her smile nothing short of naughty. "You want to make a margarita out of me?"

"More like suck the juice out," he said succinctly and pushed back from his desk, patting the space in front of him. "Up you go. Let's see if you taste as good as you look."

She didn't move but her gaze went heavy with arousal as she eyed the spot on his desk. "That sounds like a recipe for getting nothing accomplished today."

"Exactly. That was always going to happen."

"Then why did we bother to come in to the office?" she asked with maddening practicality. "We could have both taken a sick day and spent the entire morning in bed."

"Now you're talking." Why hadn't that occurred to him? "We'll do that tomorrow."

But she shook her head with an amused laugh. "We can't spend two days in a row doing nothing but boinking."

"Wanna bet?" *Boinking*. It was such a cute word for sex, especially the way they did it. Laurel had gotten him so hot a couple of times that he'd devolved into nothing but animalistic instinct. "We just spent the last two days in a row doing nothing but."

"That's not true—we went shopping. And I distinctly remember a movie. Maybe there was some eating."

Why was she still talking when he'd already told her he planned to pleasure her on his desk? Maybe he hadn't made it clear what he'd meant earlier. "Do you have some objection to me putting my mouth between your legs while we're at work?"

Her gaze went molten as she zeroed in on his lips. "Yeah, actually. I do."

Despite her protest, he'd watched her come enough times over the weekend that he could tell how turned on she was. It was doing a number on him imagining how wet she must be under that lime-green skirt. He crossed his arms over his chest and leaned back.

"Really? Because your face is telling me a different story."

"Wanting something is not the same as thinking it's a good idea." She crossed her own arms over her stomach, which tightened the fabric across her breasts, highlighting her hard nipples. "We have important work to do and I'm getting the distinct feeling you're using sex to avoid it."

That put enough of a hitch in his stride that his arousal fizzled a notch. As such, he couldn't let the comment go. "What's that supposed to mean?"

"The fundraiser. We've done nothing to plan it. We haven't even had one conversation outside of the initial one where I presented the idea of an auction. Why not?" The sensual vibe in the room vanished as they stared at each other. "Because it seems an awful lot like you want me in your bed but not your boardroom."

That stung. And put his back up at the same time. "You're being ridiculous. That's not true."

Even as he said it, he couldn't fully sell it to himself, though. With considerable effort, he took a figurative step back and examined her point.

She wasn't wrong.

He hadn't fully trusted her with details about his inheritance test. Actually, he hadn't trusted her at all. He'd maybe had a couple of discussions in the hallway once upon a time, but as a whole, he'd kept tight control over the fundraising aspect of his job. Because it was *his*. He needed to prove that he could do this task, despite having no idea why it had been thrust upon him.

And maybe that was the real reason he'd yet to share any of it with Laurel. If he didn't understand why his own father had turned on him, how would he recognize it when someone he didn't know as well did the same?

Someone like Laurel.

Keeping everyone at arm's length had become his coping mechanism. Passion hadn't even come all that easily, but he'd at least been able to quantify the benefits of that. His inheritance test? Whole other story.

Laurel was calling him on his crap and he'd never been more affected by a woman in his life.

She raised her brows. "If it's not true, then help me stop feeling like you're brushing me off when it comes to the partnership we've both agreed to."

Laurel deserved that explanation and probably a whole lot more. He stood and pulled a chair around, setting it next to his, a pointed equal distance from his computer. "Let's talk."

Shooting him a smile that was far too forgiving, she skirted the desk and settled into her seat. "Did you talk to your friends about donating items?"

"A few. I got sidetracked."

A poor excuse, though he *had* been a little busy getting wound up with the woman in lime green. Before Laurel could call him on that, too, he held up a hand. "I had a hard time, okay? It didn't go very well. You helped me get my head on straight during our conversation in the conference room the other day after the orientation session, and then I never cycled back around to it. I absolutely should dive back in."

She glanced at his phone emphatically. "No time like the present."

That was fair. As a show of good faith, he picked up his phone and scrolled through the contacts. Under Laurel's watchful gaze, he dialed up Simon

Perry, the head of Metro Bank and father to Liam from the orientation session. The man answered on the second ring. Odds were high Simon had Xavier in his contacts, and he took a moment to be grateful the LeBlanc name held enough weight to warrant such attention.

"Mr. Perry," Xavier began, struck all over again by how much further along in life his acquaintance was. "Xavier LeBlanc calling."

Unnecessary to identify himself, most likely, but this call justified formality.

"A welcome surprise," Simon said warmly. "My son mentioned that he'd met you the other day. Thank you for making him feel like he can make a difference in the world. It's an important concept I've tried to impart to him and I'm glad to hear he's finding similar influences in the business world."

"My pleasure," Xavier said and meant it. How about that? There was some actual emotional satisfaction in being the head of a place like LBC. Temporary head, though that qualification was coming a lot less quickly lately. Val had once mentioned that Xavier might be a better man for his time here. Perhaps this was what he'd meant.

"What can I do for you?" Simon asked.

Xavier launched into an unrehearsed spiel about the auction and within a few minutes, Simon had offered up a rare bottle of Macallan whiskey. While not a personal fan of the brand, Xavier knew the bottle would likely sell for upward of a hundred grand. It was a phenomenal donation and he told Simon so.

They wrapped up the call after Simon tacked on a promise to send Xavier a few names of colleagues who might be willing to contribute.

"Well done," Laurel said softly when Xavier hung up.

"You don't even know how it went," he teased, even though he knew he wore a grin he couldn't quite control. Why should he, though? He'd taken her advice, done something he'd previously failed at and came out a winner this time. If that didn't warrant a smile, nothing did.

"Yes I do. I can see it in your face. It's breathtaking." Her quiet voice curled through him with warmth. Or maybe it was the content of her words that had such an unexpected effect.

"What is my face doing?" He couldn't help but ask.

"Everything. Your expression is typically very schooled. I like it better when you let me see what's going on inside you."

Since there was no point in trying to compose his features into something less revealing, he didn't bother trying. "Well, you're a limited audience of one who can actually read me with any degree of accuracy."

"I like that, too."

This whole conversation shouldn't be happening. It was far too intimate. But the real danger lay in how much more intimate he wanted to get, which should have been scaring the daylights out of him.

Instead of reeling it back, he leaned into her space and tipped up her chin to feather a kiss across her cheek that had nothing to do with getting her naked or even aroused; it was a small token of gratitude for the things he was feeling inside.

"You're good for me, apparently."

That pleased her immeasurably, judging by the light that dawned in her eyes. Maybe he was good for her, too. Wouldn't that be something?

For the first time in his adult life, he hadn't kicked a woman out of his bed and then promptly forgotten her. The uncharted waters he'd sailed into weren't as difficult to navigate as he would have guessed.

"Maybe you should make a few more phone calls while you're riding high," Laurel suggested wryly, intentionally moving out of his reach.

Yeah, yeah, it was getting too mushy in here for both of them. He got it. Plus she'd already called him out once for his avoidance tactics. Neither did he want to scare her away simply because he'd discovered something new and amazing.

He could wait to show her how much he appreciated her.

Twelve

Auction day started at five in the morning.

Xavier didn't typically get up this early on a Saturday, but he and Laurel had a to-do list a quadrillion items long. Even though they'd recruited as many volunteers from LBC as possible, the list never got shorter and Adelaide, who had turned out to be his second-greatest asset after Laurel, had to run the food pantry while they were off-site.

Xavier drove the truck they'd rented while Laurel rode shotgun, chattering a mile a minute about the changes she'd made to the catering menu. He listened with half an ear, not because her comments weren't important, but because he'd gotten more and more nerve-racked the closer they got to the venue.

This was it. The event they'd been planning for

a solid two weeks. What if it didn't go as well as they'd projected?

Sure the appraised value of the donations had topped three million dollars, but only for insurance purposes. Actual value might not even turn out to be half that. It all depended on whether the attendees opened their wallets. Scratch that—it all depended on how wide Xavier convinced them to open their wallets.

What if *he* was the reason it failed?

Worse, what if his father had set him up for exactly that? Instead of proving his father wrong, Xavier would be proving his father so very right.

The pressure mounted until his shoulders ached, as if the weight across them had real substance.

"I can feel you panicking," Laurel said into the silence, reading his mind.

"*Panic* is a strong word," he responded mildly.

"And when you start using your 'nothing's bothering me' tone, I have to believe *panic* is the right word." Her hand slid across his thigh and squeezed, imparting comfort and understanding. "Of course, if you don't want me to guess, you could always tell me what's going on."

The traffic light ahead of him turned red, but he waited until he'd come to a complete stop before answering her.

"I'm panicking, okay?" He scowled. Boy, he was really inspiring confidence here, in both of them. "I don't know why. I shouldn't be."

Her hand smoothed over his thigh again. "Because this is important to you. There's nothing wrong with that."

"But there is something wrong with letting it affect me. I can't fail today."

"You won't," she said fiercely enough to make him do a double take. "*We* won't. I'm here and we're going to do this thing together. Haven't you figured that out by now?"

Yeah. Maybe. Mostly, anyway.

After everything she'd said, all the conversations, the proof that she was aboveboard, there was still a part of him that automatically held back. He had to consciously loosen his grip on his worries, and sometimes that didn't go so well. It wasn't a crime. They were taking things slowly, or at least he was taking *that* part slowly. If she didn't like it, too bad.

"Why are you so invested in this, anyway? It's my deal," he grumbled, well aware that his nerves were causing him to be crabby.

He'd thrown that question in her direction strictly to change the subject, but now that it was out there, he realized it had been bothering him. They'd worked twelve hour days, even on the weekends. She had literally no skin in this game other than volunteering for the job.

"That's why, silly," she said with a smile, as if that should have been perfectly obvious. "You need me. Poof. Here I am."

He didn't deserve her loyalty, especially not when he was still deliberately holding back.

"But you don't even know why it's so critical," he

blurted out and immediately wished he could recall the words. She was too sharp to let it pass.

His inheritance test was a can of worms he'd yet to open with her, and he'd just pulled into the lot of the hotel where they'd taken over one of the ballrooms. They had an enormous amount of work to do in order to get the venue decorated and ready for the auction, which would take place at eight o'clock sharp.

Not only did they have to transform the ballroom, they'd opted for black tie, which meant they both also had to change out of their T-shirts and jeans at some point. He didn't have time to get into the details of the inheritance test with her. And he really didn't want to have a conversation about why he hadn't told her about it already.

She cocked her head. "You mean, there's another objective besides the obvious?"

"Yeah." Now he had yet another reason not to go down this path—thus far, she'd apparently assumed he was fired up over fundraising strictly for altruistic reasons. And he didn't want to disappoint her. "Can we talk about it later?"

"Sure," she said immediately, and that made him feel even worse.

He had to tell her the truth. He owed it to her, if for no other reason than because she *did* have skin in the game: her time, her efforts, her faith in him. But also because this was where the rubber met the road. If he wanted to practice letting go of things and showing Laurel that he trusted her, this was what trust looked like. He had to lay out everything, even the ugly parts, and hope she didn't leap from the truck in disgust.

"Is this the part where I'm allowed to yell at you for being so understanding?" he asked. When her mouth quirked up, he returned the smile almost automatically. It was like a reflex; Laurel smiled and it made him happy. "My father's will…it's a little unconventional. Val and I had to switch places as a stipulation in order to get our inheritances."

"Oh." She drew the word out to about ten syllables. "*That's* why—"

"There's more." He hated interrupting, but he might not get this out if he had to wait. "I have to raise ten million dollars or I don't get a dime."

"That's ridiculous," Laurel returned immediately. "An inheritance shouldn't come with strings. What in the world did your father hope to accomplish by attaching fundraising to his will? It's not like he's around to see whether you succeed or not."

"Well…yeah. Exactly." Was he supposed to feel so relieved that she got it? That she'd latched onto the real culprit in all of this instead of lambasting Xavier for being so shallow? "I know diamonds. Not fundraising. It's been tripping me up to be so far out of my element."

"You listen to me, Xavier," she said sternly and slid her fingers through his hair to cup the back of his head, holding him in place so she could speak directly to him. "You're doing spectacular at fundraising. You're amazing and you've got this. We'll get your ten million dollars come hell or high water.

If this auction doesn't do it, we'll keep going until we get there. I'm just mad enough on your behalf to dig my heels in."

"That's it?" he asked and couldn't even care that his incredulity was likely plastered across his face. Of all the possible reactions she could have had, that one was not even on his list. "You're all-in even knowing that I'm doing this for purely materialistic reasons?"

She flicked that question away with her hand as if it was a bothersome insect and shook her head. "You're not doing this for the money and there's not one single thing you can say to make me believe that you are. Your father insulted you, maybe even hurt you. You want to get back at him by succeeding. I get it."

"Uh, yeah, I guess you do." Dazed, he stared at her as something monumental shifted in his chest, making room for Laurel to settle inside as if she'd always been there. "Where did you *come* from?"

"Springfield," she said with a laugh. "Born and raised. I only came to Chicago to go to college and then I sort of stuck around."

He couldn't do anything else in that moment but grab her up in a fierce kiss, one she eagerly responded to. If they hadn't been in the cab of a panel truck, he'd have been stripping her at this very moment, determined to get to that place where she made him feel whole.

Hell, she was doing that right now, even dressed. For the first time, he fully believed he could complete this inheritance test. Laurel would stand by his side until he did. What more could he ask for?

The auction was a rousing success from the first moment to the last. Of course, it couldn't have been anything less given the involvement of LBC's staff, who had donated their own items handcrafted with love. As the master of ceremonies, Xavier had been magnificent. So much so, Laurel hadn't been able to peel her eyes from his gorgeous form all night.

Especially now, with his black tie unbound and hanging around his neck as he directed a couple of the volunteers who were removing the giant banner over the raised dais where the auctioneer had led the festivities.

Though dozens of people still milled through the ballroom, Xavier caught her watching him and slid her a secret grin that might mean any number of things, but she hoped it was an indicator of how thrilled he was with the outcome of the auction. As he should be.

Once the banner came down, he extracted himself from the volunteers and somehow managed to maneuver her into a private corner, where the foot traffic wasn't as heavy.

"The auction went far better than I had a right to expect," he said as he gathered her close in a celebratory hug that quickly grew into something more precious than air.

She let herself be swallowed by the enormous rush of emotions for about five seconds and then wormed out of his embrace. With regret. It was always hard to stop touching him, regardless of the location. But the longer she stayed in his arms, the more she wanted to whisper the things in her heart.

"There are way too many LBC staffers still here to be getting so cozy," she reminded him pointedly. They still hadn't announced to the world that they were dating.

Bold, brave Laurel had taken what she'd wanted and been richly rewarded over and over again for far longer than she would have expected. She kept waiting for everything to come to an immediate and abrupt halt when he told her he was through exploring.

"Then we should go home," he murmured, heat leaping into his gaze so fast that it made her dizzy.

Things *never* came to an abrupt halt because he kept saying stuff like that.

Home, as in his house. The place she'd started subconsciously calling home, as well. But it wasn't hers, no matter how hard he tried to make her comfortable there. Neither did she dare fall prey to the seductive idea that he might eventually ask her to stay permanently.

They weren't doing permanent. They were doing hot, uninhibited and adventurous. Nothing else, no matter how many times she found herself straying off in a fantasy that had a different end.

"Don't we still have work to do?" she countered breathlessly, as he treated her to a hungry once-over that affected her almost as strongly as it would have if he'd used his hands. Maybe more so because he wasn't touching her. They were in public and he couldn't. That somehow made it more delicious, more arousing.

"There's only one thing I want to do right now, and it has nothing to do with the auction," he told her. His low voice snaked through her, heating everything in its path. "We've been here almost all day. We have volunteers for a reason."

"I can't argue with that logic."

Before the entire sentence had left her mouth, he was steering her toward the door, murmuring wicked things in her ear until she shuddered. The valet had his Aston Martin waiting in the lane by the time they arrived at the curb, even though he'd driven the rental truck—a trick that she had no clue how he'd performed, but that she appreciated, especially when he threw the car into gear impatiently.

She'd learned to gauge exactly how turned on he was by the way he drove, and the screech of his tires around a corner said he was nearly thermonuclear.

Good. So was she.

They still hadn't explored the foyer, nor had he made good on his promise to back her up against a stone column, but she didn't mind. His bed worked for her. *He* worked for her.

Within seconds of hitting the threshold of his bedroom, he'd lifted the hem of her dress over her head and pulled her onto the mattress, twining their bodies together until she scarcely knew which way was up.

Then it didn't matter as he plunged her into a

netherworld of sensation where only the two of them existed. Xavier drove her body to the heights of pleasure, wrung so much feeling from her very soul that she nearly sobbed with relief when she came. As he followed her, she clung tightly to his shoulders, anchoring herself lest she float away.

The longer she did this, the less certain she was about whether she'd walk away unscathed. But she'd agreed to help Xavier explore passion and she couldn't just stop cold turkey because she'd started assigning more importance to their relationship than she should.

This wasn't the precursor to something long term. It couldn't be—she hadn't told him the truth about who she was and she didn't believe for a second that they were headed to a place where she needed to. They were sleeping together because they both enjoyed it and one day, that would stop being true. He'd even said they were helping each other be bold.

Plus, she'd pretty much decided that her story about the fraud was a no-go since she hadn't found any evidence. Besides, Xavier made her feel like she could focus on her flagging career and successfully find another story to break that would fix her mortifying gaff. She'd be better for her time with him and look back on it fondly.

But that's all there was to this.

It was just…when he snuggled her close and stroked his strong fingers through her hair, it didn't *feel* like they were winding down. She spent every night in his bed and they'd worked on the auction for hours upon hours outside of bed, yet she never got tired of being with him. Surely that meant something. But what, she couldn't wrap her head around.

"I still can't believe that Miro painting went for 1.4 million dollars," Xavier commented out of the blue as his lips toyed with her hair. "*One* piece fetched what I had braced myself to accept as the sum total of *all* the donations."

"You're the one who drove the price up," she reminded him, relieved to jump on something that would pull her away from the angst and drama in her own head. "It was like you'd been auctioneering your whole life when you got up on stage and announced to the audience that there were two collectors in the crowd, then got them bidding against each other."

He shrugged modestly, his muscles rippling against her back and shoulders. "Helps that I knew so many people in attendance."

"Yes, it does. Whatever your father's posthumous game is with that will, it's not going to keep you from your inheritance."

Laurel could at least help give him that satisfaction before they ended this. At this point, she'd all but abandoned the idea of uncovering anything problematic at LBC. Not on purpose. She'd just been so busy with the auction that investigating had slipped in priority. Okay, maybe the slip had been a little more on purpose than she'd let herself admit. If she didn't investigate, she didn't have to worry about how to bring it up with Xavier, nor did she have to worry about making any mistakes.

"If all the money comes in from the auction as expected, I should be pretty close to the ten million," he said.

"If you want, I can meet with Addy and someone from accounting on Monday to get some solid numbers."

"Sure." Xavier mouthed down her neck to her shoulder, then lower, ratcheting up the intensity within seconds. Her body bowed beneath his talented lips as he worshipped one of her breasts, and she forgot all about the auction.

It wasn't until Monday morning, after she'd already taken a seat between Addy and Michelle from accounting, that it occurred to her that this was precisely the position she'd hoped to be in when she'd taken the job: trusted enough to be given access to LBC's books.

Her pulse drummed in her throat the entire time Addy and Michelle talked her through the numbers. Nothing calmed her ragged nerves, not even the news that Xavier was, indeed, very close to the ten-million-dollar mark. If he hosted another successful fundraiser, he'd hit his goal easily, as best she could tell from the preliminary figures.

That meant he might cut her loose soon and that hit her hard. She couldn't keep pretending that everything was going to work out fine, not when the thought of losing him hurt so deeply that she couldn't make it stop. It all seemed to be coming to a head but she couldn't see what the next steps were.

Laurel asked Michelle when she could check back to get final numbers and then scribbled out a few ideas Addy had for another fundraiser. The three women chatted and then Michelle and Addy segued into an entirely different conversation about a problem with the meal services area that apparently had been going on for some time.

Laurel listened with half an ear as she added her own notes to Addy's thoughts. The auction had been so successful because they'd heavily involved the staff and there was no reason to change that. In fact, Laurel wanted to take it a step further and involve the staff's families.

"Jennifer has been off with her estimates for so long, no one even thinks twice about it," Michelle said to Addy, flicking her fingers dismissively at the computer screen open in front her.

"Oh, I know." Addy rolled her eyes. "Marjorie used to complain about it twice a month, when Jennifer submitted her budget and then again when she submitted her expenses. I don't know why Jennifer bothers to come up with a budget at all."

"It's only because I make her," Michelle said with a laugh. "If I had to approve her expenditures, I'd go insane trying to match them to her budget. I'm more than happy to let Val handle that."

Laurel tried really, really hard to ignore the way her spine tingled. But it was no use. She'd heard every word and her vast experience with human na-

ture told her there was more to this story than had
been expressed thus far.

"Val approves all the invoices from the meal services area? Not someone in accounting?" Laurel
asked.

"Yeah," Michelle offered readily. "Or he did.
Xavier does now, because of the amount. LBC has
a rule about who can approve over a certain dollar
threshold."

Which wasn't uncommon. But it was somewhat
irregular for no one to reconcile the budgeted amount
to the actual spend, which didn't seem to be happening. Nor had anyone done anything about the dis-
crepancy, if it extended as far back as when both Val
and Marjorie had been involved.

Laurel tucked that information away, opting not to
press Michelle on it since there was no evidence of
any wrongdoing. Except, as the day wore on, Laurel
couldn't quite dismiss the whole thing. Her original
sources had mentioned discrepancies with accounting for items stocked in the supply closet, not with
the meal services area, but who was to say there
weren't issues in more than one area? Or it could be
that there were no problems at all and all of this was
unfounded suspicion that would be easily disproved.

That's what she'd come here to find out.

Either way, it was time to bring Xavier up to speed
on what she'd heard. It was exactly what she'd promised herself she'd do if and when something like this
came up. It would be a great test of his intentions toward her and definitely would reveal whether they

were moving toward something better than what she'd braced for.

This whole matter would be decided, once and for all.

Thirteen

When Laurel appeared at the door of Xavier's office after a very long morning apart, the look on her face immediately eliminated the idea that she'd been thinking about him in a wholly non-work-related way. Which meant he couldn't boost her up on the desk and push her skirt to her waist like *he'd* been thinking about.

"Is this a business visit?" he asked, just in case he'd misread things.

She nodded and shut the door. Xavier closed his laptop and crossed his arms, though it was a sure bet neither would prevent him from angling for a way to get her onto the desk in a few minutes.

"I talked to Michelle in accounting a little while ago," she began and then hesitated.

His throat tightened as he recalled that Laurel had mentioned she'd ask for the fundraising numbers today. Surely he wasn't *that* far behind his ten-million-dollar goal. "Why doesn't your expression look like the news is good? I'm not that bad at math. I can't be more than a couple of million off."

"Oh, yeah, no, you're not." She waved that away, obviously startled that he'd mentioned it, as if fundraising hadn't even crossed her mind. "You're right on track. We just need one more good event like the auction and you're all set. Addy and I already hashed out some preliminary ideas that I'll run by you sometime."

"Okay, good. Why does that not make me feel better?"

She flashed a brief grin that warmed his insides, and that did make him feel better. As long as she kept smiling like that, nothing could go wrong.

"While I was talking to Michelle, some other stuff came up. About the accounting for the meal services area. I…" Laurel made a face. "Well, I hate to speculate, so I'm just going to tell you what she said and let you draw your own conclusions. Apparently there's a running joke that the manager of that area can't hit her budget. She's constantly over in her expenditures but no one has asked for an explanation."

A decade of monthly meetings where he'd scoured the balance sheet at LeBlanc rushed into his head in an instant and it was all he could do to remain calm. "You suspect fraud."

It wasn't a question, and the brief, bright flash

in her gaze told him everything he needed to know. The calm he usually called up easily when dealing with the unexpected wouldn't surface.

"I don't know *anything*," she said simply, which didn't settle his stomach. "Only that Michelle mentioned that Val approves that area's expenses. And now you do."

"Okay." He had to start digging. Right now. "I hear you. This is my mess to clean up."

His stomach sloshed a bit more when she didn't immediately insist they were in this together or lean on the desk with fire in her eyes as she demanded that he let her be his clean-up partner. He couldn't focus on how much he wished she had, not when there was a potential issue festering beneath the surface of LeBlanc Charities.

If someone was stealing from LBC on Xavier's watch, there would be hell to pay. Then he could worry about why it felt like Laurel was slipping away.

Many long, grueling hours later, he and Michelle had run through enough of the numbers enough times to be convinced they'd only scratched the surface of the problem. The head of accounting had worn a sick expression on her face for the whole of the meeting. Xavier was pretty sure that same look had been etched on his.

"It's late," he told her and glanced at the clock, not at all shocked to see that it was past eight. "You should go home. I'll hire an independent audit firm in the morning to do a thorough excavation of the disarray our books are in."

And he meant "our" in every sense of the word. He'd signed off on some of the receipts and invoices, which appeared to have been inflated above their actual amounts. This was his to fix.

"Thank you for not firing me," she said quietly, her gratitude evident. "This should have been caught a long time ago."

"It's not all on you. Marjorie had a role in this, as does Val." Not to mention Jennifer Sanders, the manager of the meal services area who, it appeared, had been skimming off the top of LBC's operating capital for quite some time and rather blatantly, too. "I would ask that you keep this to yourself until we have enough evidence to bring up charges."

That was the real reason he hadn't fired anyone yet. He needed facts before acting, and he couldn't trust the rage that seethed just under his skin. Until he had rock-solid proof from an unbiased third party about what had been happening, and for how long, he couldn't blame anyone 100 percent. Though Val topped his list at this moment.

His brother had some explaining to do.

Michelle slipped into a brown leather coat to brave Chicago's fall weather, then left without a backward glance. Xavier was too keyed up to go home, where Laurel was no doubt waiting for him, though he hadn't had a chance to really speak to her since she'd brought him the news that LBC wasn't being run as tightly as it could be.

He sent her a text message that was short and to the point: Don't wait on me for dinner.

Then he drove down by the lake, though the scenery wasn't all that pretty this time of year. Closer to New Year's, the trees would be bare of leaves and ice would form in large chunks on the shore. When the water froze, the lake looked like a giant sheet of glass, a testament to the power of an Illinois winter. That was his favorite. Tonight, the lake was choppy and dark and there was no moon to light the water.

He wanted to go home, despite how angry and heartsick he was over the suspected fraud. The problem was that he was even more heartsick over not understanding the reasons Laurel had basically dumped this in his lap and backed away. Was it because her role in his life was temporary and they were almost done? Maybe she wondered why she should get involved.

It wasn't that he wished for her to solve his problems. Only that he wished they were partners in this, too. That they could be partners in everything.

And he wished he could bring that up with her. It was too soon. He couldn't rush things.

Instead of heading for Val's house in River Forest, which was where he should be going, Xavier found himself on the North Shore. On a whim, he pulled up to the gate of his mother's neighborhood. The attendant nodded the moment he recognized Xavier and opened the gate to admit him, though he hadn't visited his mother since Thanksgiving last year. She wasn't expecting him.

If anyone would have some advice about how to handle this problem with LBC, it would be its founder. His mother answered the door of the palatial mansion herself, swinging one of the double doors wide as he came up the marble stairs. He hadn't even had a chance to knock.

"Xavier, what in the world are you doing here?" she asked, concern tightening her mouth. "Is everything okay?"

Patrice LeBlanc could pass for forty-five all day long and wore her ash-blond hair in a timeless style that women half her age envied. He studied his mother for a moment, struck all at once by the fact that that she'd run LBC by herself for a number of years until Val had joined her.

He hadn't fully appreciated the effort that had required until this moment. "Hi, Mom. I think we should talk."

She lifted her brows but didn't comment, ushering him into the salon she preferred. The sunny yellow always made her smile, as she'd gladly tell anyone who would listen. She didn't do so this evening, opting to take a seat on one of the brocade couches.

"You're scaring me, darling," his mom finally said as he settled into the leather chair at a right angle to the couch, though he knew she'd prefer it if he sat next to her.

They'd never been close. He'd been his father's son from an early age, while she'd favored Val, openly and unapologetically. Once upon a time, he'd been pretty jealous of the easy rapport she had with his brother, but he'd gotten over it, turning his slavish devotion to his father. Look where that had gotten him.

"Sorry, I didn't mean to drop in on you completely unannounced."

"Don't be silly. You're welcome here any time of day or night."

She meant it, too. How about that? He couldn't recall a time when he'd felt overly welcome at the house his parents shared before his father had died, but maybe that was on him. He hadn't tried to form any kind of bond with his mother, just retreated into his own misery over his father's will. Maybe it was time to change that.

"How are you doing, Mom?"

She laughed nervously. "Now you're really scaring me."

Because he didn't make a habit of asking after her health, emotional or physical, which shamed him more than he liked to admit. "It just occurred to me that I haven't given much regard to how lonely you must be with Dad gone."

The look on her face pretty well matched the confusion going on beneath his own skin. Where had that *come* from? But even as he asked that silent question, he answered it.

Laurel.

She'd opened up so many channels of emotion inside him, unlocking things he'd never considered before, things he didn't know existed or that he'd care about.

But he knew now.

"That's sweet of you to ask, darling. I'm doing okay, considering." She wagged her head back and forth. "Your father and I were married for nearly thirty-five years. It's hard to be alone. But I'm managing. Why did you really come by?"

He had to chuckle at her directness, which reminded him of his father for some odd reason. He'd have never said they were at all alike. But neither would he have claimed that about himself and Laurel. And he'd have been wrong.

"I uncovered some accounting issues at LBC. Looks like someone is stealing from us using fake invoices and receipts. I'm pretty upset."

"As you should be!"

Anger swept through his mother's expression, taking over her whole body, and she looked so much like Val in that moment that Xavier did a double take. That was the kind of passion he'd equate with his brother, all right, the same kind of all-in that Xavier had always avoided, with calculation. Hot heads didn't get results.

But he'd abandoned his emotion-free state in favor of a seductive lure in the form of Laurel Dixon. She'd enticed him to jump, holding her hand, as they soared into a free fall together. And as his reward? He would eventually be as alone as his mother, and he was suddenly very aware of how much he didn't want that.

"Tell me everything," his mother demanded, visibly bristling. "I might be retired, but my name is still LeBlanc."

Despite the somberness of the subject, that made

him smile even as he laid out what he knew. Xavier
concluded with the news that he'd already contacted
an audit firm who specialized in nonprofit-sector accounting. His mother nodded and laid out a few of
her own thoughts, namely that he needed to involve
Val as soon as possible.

"I appreciate that you came to me first instead
of Val," she told him. "It's a real testament to how
far you've come since the reading of your father's
will. I was against the idea of forcing you and your
brother to switch places, at first, but Edward talked
me into it."

"Why?" he blurted out, aching to understand once
and for all why his father had hated him so much.
"What possible good could have resulted from these
ridiculous inheritance terms?"

"Darling." She shook her head, piercing him with
a look that said he should have already figured this
out. "If you hadn't been deep in the heart of LBC,
would this theft have come to light? Would you have
ever darkened my door? Your father worried that
you were becoming too much like him and he didn't
want you to get to the end of your life, only to have
the same regrets he had."

Regrets? Over building an almost billion-dollar-a-
year company? Something did not add up here. "Are
you saying that Dad did this because *he* had regrets?"

But as she nodded, he couldn't summon a shred
of anger. His mother was right; none of this would
have happened if Xavier had stayed locked in his office at LeBlanc Jewelers.

Laurel wouldn't have happened.

And if he hadn't let her into his life, she might never have brought this theft to his attention. It had been the best combination of fate and design, but only by putting his trust in her had he gotten here.

"Sure. Regrets about not spending more time with Val, regrets about teaching you to be so hard, regrets about not traveling the world with me when he had the chance." His mother lifted a shoulder. "He had many."

Xavier would not have described himself as *hard*, at least, not prior to being propelled into LBC. LeBlanc Jewelers required a firm hand and, apparently, so did LBC, which he could provide. But he'd also learned that there were people at the cores of both enterprises that he'd overlooked—some of them, like Adelaide, to his detriment.

After standing at the helm of a charity for the last few months, he could at least take an objective step back and wonder if there was still more truth to uncover. Especially the one thing that still bothered him about all of this.

"If Dad did this to help me, where does Val fit into his master plan?"

His mother didn't miss a beat. "Val has his own challenges, namely that he cares too much. He needs to learn how mix objectivity with his tendency to lead with his heart. Your father thought both he and LeBlanc Jewelers would benefit from the switch. I think he was right."

Xavier ran a hand through his hair and tried to

make some sense out of his reeling thoughts. The will *hadn't* been a blunt instrument designed to wreck both Val's and Xavier's carefully constructed lives, if his mom could be believed.

He believed her.

And that meant he no longer defaulted to not trusting anyone, up to and including his family.

If he took anything from this conversation, it was that nothing was as it seemed. Which meant he had some more thinking to do about *all* of his next steps, not just the ones associated with the accounting issues at LBC.

He couldn't keep holding Laurel at arm's length and neither could he let her go.

It was far past time to admit he'd fallen in love with her.

When Xavier blew through the door of his bedroom and snatched Laurel up in a fierce embrace, she scarcely had time to yelp before he'd swallowed her whole with the most mind-altering kiss she'd experienced from him yet.

His hands were everywhere, in her hair, slicking down her back, holding her so tightly that she couldn't imagine being separated.

And they were still dressed. She didn't have enough working brain cells to question him about his meeting with Michelle, whether he'd eaten or what occasion had prompted such a display of raw need. She just let herself be taken by the storm until he finally pulled back and rested his forehead on hers.

"Hi," he murmured with a small smile.

Dragging in great big quantities of air, she scratched out her own *"Hi"* in response.

He followed that with, "I missed you."

Oh, God. She'd missed him, too, pacing up and down the length of the study downstairs that smelled like him, the best combination of man and sandalwood. Eventually she'd wandered back to his bedroom to bury her face in his pillow.

It shouldn't have been such a big deal to miss one night together, especially not when he'd been contending with the accounting issue. But they'd spent 24/7 in each other's company for weeks. Without him around, she'd fallen into withdrawal, seeking out anything she could find to give her even a small hit of Xavier.

And here he was, rocking her from the inside out with nothing more than a few simple words.

"I gathered something of the sort," she managed to get out. "I hope it was okay that I waited here at your house—"

"I wanted you to. In fact, I want you here all the time." He cupped her jaw, feathering his thumb across her lips. "Move in. Tomorrow. Let's make this official."

Yes. Yes, yes, yes.

Yes to discovering what it felt like to love him wholly and completely. Yes to exploring what they could mean to each other. Yes to—

Oh, no. *No.*

Her throat closed so fast that she saw stars. A

monumental weight dropped down on her chest as she struggled to extract herself from his grip. This *could not* be happening before she'd had a chance to tell him the truth. He finally let her go, ruefully rubbing the back of his neck as he stared down at her.

"Too fast?" he asked with a half laugh. "I practiced what I was going to say on the way home from my mom's house. It kind of all rushed out, so I'm sorry if I messed it up."

"You, um…" He'd gone to his mother's house? Strictly to work out how to upend her entire world or for another reason entirely? Her head spun. "You didn't mess up. At least, I don't think you did. What exactly are you saying?"

"I'm saying I'm falling for you, Laurel."

And with that one single devastating phrase, everything came apart. Her soul. Her plans. Her sanity.

"You can't drop that on me," she whispered, even as her heart greedily latched onto the idea that Xavier LeBlanc had just admitted he was *falling for her*. "Not now."

"When, then?" Confusion marred his beautiful face, which made the swirl in her stomach worse. "I don't hear you saying you don't feel the same. What's holding us back?"

The truth.

"The fact that you don't know who I really am," she burst out, wishing with all her might that she'd already told him so she could admit she'd fallen for him, too.

This wasn't supposed to be happening, not like this.

He took a step back, his expression veering between such a wide range of emotions that she couldn't sort them all. "What are *you* saying?"

"That's what I'm trying to explain! Give me a minute to get my feet under me."

She took a deep breath. It didn't help. She still had no clue how to approach this conversation other than to jump and hope he took her hand on the way down.

Please, God, let that be what happens.

She wanted Xavier more than she wanted to breathe and it was all within her grasp. Or it never was and she'd ruined everything prior to even walking through the door of LBC by choosing not to reveal her true profession.

"I'm an investigative reporter," she said bluntly and prayed he'd take it with the spirit she'd intended. "I took the job at LBC to uncover the fraud I suspected was going on. I'm sorry. I should have told you sooner."

"But you didn't," he said slowly. "Why not?"

"I tried to! In the conference room. You interrupted me at least four times—"

"And I've kept a muzzle over your mouth every minute since then?"

"I didn't think we were serious, Xavier. I never expected to have a reason to mention it after that. But then I got into this with you so much deeper than I planned. I wanted to tell you, but I never found solid evidence until today. And then you blew in here and things got all jumbled up."

In that respect, he *had* moved too fast. But it was

too late and she couldn't blame him, not when it was all her fault.

"Let me get this straight." He pinched the bridge of his nose, his eyes closed in apparent disbelief. "You aren't a fundraising wizard and you've been toying with me this whole time."

"No! Oh, my God, no." Horrified, she reached out without thinking and then flinched when he jerked out of her grasp. "Why would you think I was toying with you? I have done fundraising in the past. That part is true, just like the way I feel about you. Everything between us is real."

"Nothing between us is real," he corrected harshly. "I don't trust a single word coming out of your mouth right now."

"Xavier." She bit back at least four different trite phrases, all designed to prove her innocence, which wasn't fair. She wasn't innocent. "You're right, and I'm sorry. I shouldn't have hidden my reasons for being at LBC. But you're missing the most important part of this. I'm not going to do the story on the accounting discrepancies. That's why I told you about it. I changed my mind."

"Thank you for your generosity," he said flatly. "I plan to press charges against the likely suspect as soon as I get the proper evidence. If you'd broken the story in advance of that, she might have had time to cover her tracks. So we'll call it even. I won't fire you for taking the job under false pretenses and you'll turn in your resignation to Adelaide first thing in the morning."

Oh, God. He wasn't going to give her a second chance. Her heart tore in two and lay there in pieces, bleeding.

"That's it, then?" she asked in disbelief.

She didn't have to wait for his nod. She'd screwed up again, even though she'd been trying to do the right thing.

"What would you like me to say? Apparently we weren't that serious and I misunderstood our relationship."

His voice had taken on that quality she hated, the one that he adopted to make sure everyone understood he was above the petty emotions swirling through the room. Nothing fazed him.

Except she knew better. "I *wanted* it to be serious. I just didn't…"

There wasn't a good way to end that sentence.

"You didn't what? Think I deserved the truth? Think I'd find out? Think I'd care?" His gaze bored into hers. "I did. To all three."

Past tense. She got the message loud and clear. He didn't care anymore. And he was done with her at the exact moment that she figured out what she wanted—Xavier.

"Okay. I get that you're angry—"

"I'm not angry. I'm ambivalent, at best," he said with a shrug. "You can clear all of your things out of my house at your convenience. I won't be here."

With that, he calmly walked out the door, leaving her trembling in the middle of his bedroom wondering how she could have been so colossally stupid as to lose both the story and the guy in one shot.

Fourteen

Xavier ended up driving to Val's house, after all. There was nowhere else to go and he'd developed this eerie calm that had started to scare him.

After weeks of consciously letting go, of allowing himself to roll around in sensations and experiences, he couldn't seem to feel anything at all.

A blessing, really. Laurel *had* been hiding something from him. A pretty big something. She was a liar—and a really good one, at that. All this time, he'd taken the fall for his suspicions, blaming his father's will for instilling this inconvenient sense of caution that he'd had to work on overcoming. In reality, Laurel had been undercover, scheming to break open a scandal starring LeBlanc Charities. *On Xavier's watch*, no less.

He wanted to hate her. To bask in his righteous indignation. To wallow in his justifications for walking away from her. But he couldn't feel anything other than numb.

When he got to Val's, it was well past midnight. Probably because he'd taken the long way around via Naperville. He shouldn't go inside Val's house. If there was a prize for least-fit company, Xavier would win it. Given his mood, the last person he should be speaking to was Val when they hadn't hashed out the Jennifer Sanders problem yet.

Just as he hit the start button to gun the engine so he could jet out of there, Val materialized at the car's driver's-side door and tapped on the glass.

Xavier slid down the window. "What?"

"Laurel called me," Val explained without fanfare.

Val hadn't found it necessary to take Xavier to task for his snippy tone, so Laurel must have told him everything. Xavier sighed. He was the one in his brother's driveway disturbing an entire household when everyone had to work tomorrow. The least he could do was have the courtesy to let Val explain how someone could have been robbing LBC blind for months without the director's knowledge.

Xavier peeled out of the car and slammed the door, which didn't help his mood, and followed Val into the dimly lit house.

"Sabrina's asleep," Val whispered. "I'd like to keep it that way, since she's sleeping for two."

"Yeah, yeah." Rub it in his face that Val had it all

figured out in the romance department while Xavier had literally been sleeping with the enemy.

Or the potential enemy. If she'd broken the story. Which she hadn't because... He didn't know why. Not enough evidence or something. Maybe Laurel had hoped Xavier would spill the beans to her after sex one night, once she'd gotten him good and pliant.

She wasn't like that. He knew she wasn't. Except she'd lied to him. Repeatedly. Was any of it real?

Wearily, he sank into a chair and let his head fall into his hands. He had to move on and stop thinking about her. Massaging his forehead, he glanced up at Val from under his fingers. "Start talking."

"I know Jennifer's skimming. I've known for months," Val said with a nonchalant shrug that belied the bomb he'd just dropped. "Her husband is dying of stage-four colon cancer and they're struggling to pay the bills. You know how insurance is these days. High deductibles and such. She won't take money from me. I tried to give it to her. Tell me what you'd do in that situation."

"None of that," Xavier countered immediately. "Letting employees steal from you is not how you run a profitable business. I'd fire her and let her lie in the bed she made."

And that was likely the very reason his father had conceived the inheritance switch. His mother's words flooded his mind and he flinched. Maybe *hard* was a better word to describe him than he'd been willing to admit.

"That's a crap answer, Z." Val raised his eyebrows, likely in deference to the fact that he hadn't called Xavier by his childhood nickname in many years. "That's Dad talking. What would *you* do?"

"I don't know," he mumbled as he thought about his mother being alone now and how horrible it must be to have to watch your husband die, knowing there was nothing you could do to stop it. That's why it was better never to trust in something as fleeting and unreliable as another human being.

It was too late to stop the subtle and powerful internal shifts, though. He'd already started thinking with his heart and knew he wouldn't fire the woman, though it would be within his power to do so as the acting director of LBC.

"Until you have an answer, don't press charges," Val suggested quietly. "Marjorie had a back door where she handled the accounting discrepancies, so we're okay on the audit front. I can get you details."

Of course Marjorie had been in on it. She would have to be, since the accounting manager, Michelle, had known nothing of this. And he had a feeling the independent audit firm would find exactly what Val had just told him. They were totally in the clear from a legal standpoint. Ethically, maybe not. But he could make an argument that Jennifer's judgment was impaired and thus she was not worthy of discipline.

"I'll sleep on it." *Alone*, apparently. And for some reason, the sudden image of his empty bed crawled through him, opening doors that had been shut so far this evening. The most profound sense of sadness weighed down everything, and that was the only excuse he could come up with for the reason he blurted out, "Laurel and I broke up."

Val just nodded, his expression troubled. "I know, she told me that part, too."

Was nothing sacred around here? "All of it? Like how she lied about everything?"

"All of it, like how much she loves working for LBC and how she wants to walk away from reporting. She asked if I could possibly forgive her deception and see a way to keep her on board after you go back to LeBlanc Jewelers."

Oh. She'd called to beg Val for her job. Probably she had done so strictly to curry Val's favor, since he'd be the one she'd be working for in the long term.

"You said yes," Xavier guessed grimly. "I suppose you also told her it was okay if she worked there in the interim, too."

Why not? It would be fun and games to continue working with Laurel, at least as far as Val was concerned. It had been his idea to hire her in the first place, against Xavier's better judgment. He deserved a medal for not throwing that back in Val's face.

"That's your call."

"I see. So I get to make the decision about whether to keep the best fundraising partner I could have dreamed up? Is that what you're saying? I'm the one who gets to decide if I'd like to feel as if I've been eviscerated every time I see her, day in and day out? I suppose it's all supposed to be easy, then. I should just decide to stop being in love with her, too." Xavier smirked at Val and then everything inside caught up with what he'd just unwittingly blurted out.

Oh, God, there came the hurt.

That's what he'd been so successfully avoiding thus far. He didn't like feeling so out of control, so raw inside. The same way he'd felt after the reading of the will, with all of the questions and lack of answers and overwhelming sense of betrayal.

Only this was worse. Laurel had tripped his radar from day one and he'd consciously forced himself to let go of his caution. He'd *purposefully* walked into her executioner's ax.

And what had she done? Smiled at him as she let her ax fall.

He'd *told* her how messed up he was about his father's will and she'd *understood*. Claimed to, anyway. How *dare* she say she got it when she'd been keeping secrets from him?

The rage spread, burning the raw places inside. Everything hurt. He hated it.

"I'm sorry, man," Val murmured. "I know how rough you must feel."

"What do you know about it?" he snapped back and then sighed. "Sorry. I'm messed up."

Val nodded and put a comforting hand on Xavier's shoulder. The warmth bled through his T-shirt, reminding him that he hadn't put a coat on when he'd walked out of the house.

"That's the part I know," his brother said. "I was in the opposite boat, though. Sabrina is the one who got hurt because of me and I had to fix it. I'm lucky she didn't think too hard about my flaws before accepting the ring I put on her finger, or I'd still be messed up."

"That's totally different." Also, whatever Val had done to Sabrina couldn't be nearly as bad as what Laurel had done. His brother was a saint, running a charity with flair and figuring out how to let a woman whose husband was dying pay for expensive medical treatments without losing her job or her dignity. "What did you do?"

"I hurt her." Val closed his eyes for a beat, as if the memory alone caused him pain. "We weren't serious, and then she got pregnant. I didn't shift the way I treated our relationship in time. I should have. But it happened so fast. I'd never been serious with a woman before and it was all new. I made mistakes. Fortunately, she forgave me, which, by the way, is the secret to marriage. You never stop making mistakes because it's all new, every day, if you're doing it right. As long as you go into it with forgiveness, it all works out."

"Who said anything about marriage?" Dazed, Xavier tried to take in all the things his brother had just said. "I barely even got to the point where I asked her to move in."

Val raised his brows. "Maybe that's part of your problem. You treated the entire relationship casually until *you* were ready to move forward and then didn't give Laurel enough warning to shift the way *she* thought about your relationship."

"Did she say that to you?"

What was *wrong* with him, greedily begging for scraps of information about Laurel? He should be banishing her from his mind. Except when he tried, all he could picture was her face as she pulled him down for a kiss, or her laugh, the way her voice always curled up in his gut. She'd been all-in from the beginning, charging ahead, partnering with him on a million small things that, added together, formed a woman who had given him a reason to change the core of how he dealt with relationships.

That was the thing he couldn't get over. She'd come to mean a great deal to him but he couldn't see much evidence showing she felt the same about him.

"No," Val said. "She told me that she'd screwed up the best thing that had ever happened to her and she didn't want to do that with the second-best thing. That's why she called me in hopes of salvaging her job at LBC since she'd already lost you."

"Me?" He blinked. "I'm the best thing that ever happened to her?"

"I know, it was a shock to me, as well," Val said with a smirk. "This is the part where you get back in your car and go find her so she can apologize to you directly instead of through me."

It was a testament to how befuddling this entire conversation was that Xavier almost nodded and did exactly that. But then he beat back that impulse with some heavy reminders of Laurel's treachery.

"It doesn't matter how she apologizes. There are some things that are unforgivable."

"Like stealing?" Val gave Xavier a minute to absorb that. "If you take a specific action out of context, sure. But I hope your exposure to the less fortunate has given you a different frame of mind. Motivation is complex. People make mistakes. You can seek out ways to rise above the things people do to hurt you or be alone. Your choice."

"When did you get so smart?" Xavier grumbled without any heat because, yeah, he got it.

Val just laughed. "Hey, when I sit at the head of the boardroom table at LeBlanc Jewelers, I feel like the stupidest person in the room some days. You manage that environment day in and day out with so much success that you make it look easy. So I guess I'm saying we each have our strengths, and when we put them together, we do all right. That's what Dad wanted us to figure out, you know."

If so, Xavier had played into his father's hands all along because Laurel had been the one to truly teach him that. That much had been real; he could feel the difference beneath his skin. She'd made him into a better person. And if that was true, then there might be room to reevaluate her reasons for not telling him the truth.

Xavier made a face at his brother. "I already knew that. I have no idea what took you so long."

"Then take my advice." Val punctuated that by shoving Xavier's arm until he stood up. "Go. Talk to Laurel. Don't let anything stand in the way of your happiness."

Xavier wasn't sure he could actually take that advice. Having an academic understanding that Val was probably right didn't magically make the big black bruise inside go away. Neither did he feel like he should be the one to make the effort. Laurel had been in the wrong. Not Xavier. He shouldn't have to hunt her down.

Apparently, she was of the same mind, because when he got home, she was still there, quietly sitting on his bed as if she'd been willing to patiently wait for him, even if it took all night.

"What are you doing here?" He questioned her gruffly, even as he drank in her troubled face and his soul soaked up her presence.

"Not making another mistake," she informed him, her voice doing that thing where it felt like she'd climbed inside him. "I screwed up by not telling you the truth soon enough and I'm not screwing up again."

"Then you should leave—"

"No." Slipping from the bed, she stood and faced him, her hands by her sides, though it seemed as if it took some effort to keep them there. "I need you to hear what I have to say."

He crossed his arms before he went insane and pulled her into his embrace, which was feeling more and more likely the longer she stood there within touching distance. All of this could have been avoided if he'd ensured that she'd really left the first time. Or if he'd resisted trusting her.

If she hadn't been so wonderful, so easy to be with, so amazing. Or a million other things that hadn't happened that way.

What had happened was Laurel.

She hadn't left. Apparently she wasn't going to unless he gave her the floor. "Fine. I'm listening."

Her silvery-gray eyes latched onto his, bleeding into his soul. "Xavier, I fell for you, too."

And with that, the last piece of his heart broke open and sucked him under.

Laurel's nails bit into her palms as she waited for Xavier to say something. Anything. But he just kept staring at the floor as if he'd discovered a pattern there that fascinated him. Or he couldn't bear to look at her a second longer. Either way, it meant her gamble hadn't paid off.

It was over.

She'd apologized. She'd admitted that she'd fallen in love with him, opening herself up to that single point of vulnerability, and it wasn't enough.

But then he finally glanced up, his eyes damp. That punched her in the gut. She'd hurt him and he was allowing her to witness exactly how much. What was she supposed to do with that, mourn the loss of what she could have had with him? She had been mourning it, for several long hours.

"Say that again," he demanded.

"I fell for you," she repeated succinctly, happy to have an excuse to admit it all over again. "I've never been in love before. I had no idea it would scare me so much. It made me do stupid things that I can't take back."

He nodded. "I get that. We're more alike than you might think."

Dampness sprang into her own eyes and she had to smile at what had become a running theme with them. He couldn't be too mad if he was telling jokes. There might be a thread of hope here. "Do tell."

"I've never been in love before, either, and it's making me do stupid things, too. I don't trust easily, and then you broke the fragile bit I was able to scrape together."

Oh, God, that stabbed her through the chest.

He'd *trusted* her and she'd shattered him by not telling him the truth sooner. Not breaking the story, deciding to take the evidence to him, all the small moments—none of that mattered in the end because she'd done the one thing he couldn't tolerate.

"Darling, no." She rushed it out before he could complete the last word. "Don't you dare take any of this on you. I'm the one to blame here, and it is not stupid of you to have trusted me. You have every reason to be angry and I—"

"The stupid thing I'm doing is forgiving you," he interrupted and she was so shocked, she shut up. "I'm not sure what tipped the scales but I'd rather practice getting this right with you than be alone with my self-righteousness."

Stunned, she stared at him. He was forgiving her? And wanted to be with her? None of this made a lick of sense.

"I don't understand."

"Let me spell it out, then. Laurel, I love you. Stop talking and come over here so I can show you."

Just like that. So simple and yet so complex. *I love you.*

The words penetrated into every fiber of her body until it felt like her skin would burst from the fullness inside.

Obediently, she fell into his embrace, scarcely able to credit how she was being wrapped up in Xavier LeBlanc's warm arms without having to perform seven years' penance for her sins.

"How can you just forgive me like that and not even care that I misled you?"

"I care, sweetheart," he said into her hair, his breath sensitizing her. "It's because I do care that I'm giving you another chance. If I didn't care, I'd let you go and move on easily. I've done it many times. But I don't want to not care anymore. I want to love someone enough that when they screw up, it hurts. So here's the thing I'd ask of you in exchange. Try not to screw up any more. But if you do, I'm pretty sure I can forgive that, too. Just as long as you're here being my partner at all things in life."

She laughed even as the tears started falling. "You're very gracious. You should teach a class."

"Noted. I'd rather take you to bed, if it's all the same to you."

She nodded and squealed when he picked her up, then threw her on the bed, following her down to wind her body up with his until she couldn't move.

That was perfect. If he wanted to get right to the makeup sex, that worked for her and then some.

Except…

"There's just one thing I don't understand," she said instead of kissing him senseless, which was what she should have been doing—not opening more cans of worms. "What changed between earlier tonight and now?"

Surely not her phone call to Val. Had his brother talked him into giving her another chance? If so, she owed Val about a million handwritten notes of gratitude.

"I remembered how much grace you gave me when I told you about my father's will," he muttered, color staining his cheeks. "I'd kept it from you for my own reasons and you didn't even seem to notice, just jumped right on the Xavier bandwagon, supporting me in my fundraising tasks with no questions asked. I decided I was being a little high-handed to throw away what we had solely because you hadn't yet figured out the right timing to share your guilty secret. I'm sorry."

"Did you just apologize to *me*?" Laurel choked on the phrase and not all of it came out audibly. "I'm the one who screwed up—"

"Shh. You did and you apologized." He stroked his fingertips down her face, enlivening everything under his gentle touch. "For me, this is what trust looks like, and I have to spend a lot of time getting it right. It's a concerted effort that I'm still working on. So, for now, just know that I'm over it."

"How can you say that? What if I'm lying about forty-seven other things?" She wasn't. But how could he blindly accept that?

"You forget how well we can read each other." He kissed the tip of her nose, his heart spilling all over his face. "Because we're so much alike. I'm not worried. Plus, I'm sure you'll have to forgive me on occasion when I screw up the trust thing. We'll figure it out together."

Greedily, she soaked it all up. She loved it when he let her see how much she affected him. Loved that he trusted her enough to do so. Loved him. What had she done to get so lucky as to find a man like him?

"If you can read me so well, what am I thinking about right now?" she asked, letting her heart bloom through her expression.

"A drive down the shore of Lake Michigan?" he guessed and levered one of his knees between her legs to bind them even closer together.

She snorted. "Try again."

But, instead, he just kissed her and that was exactly right. He really could read her mind.

Miraculously, Xavier was giving her the second chance she'd always craved but had never been granted. She didn't have to worry about making mistakes with him because he'd be right there with her, holding her hand as they both jumped into the unknown. Together.

Epilogue

The charity fashion show Xavier and Laurel had put together with Val and Sabrina's help started off with a bang. Literally. A glitter cannon rained sparkles onto the stage as the first model strutted down the runway dripping with LeBlanc diamonds.

This time, Xavier wasn't a nervous wreck. Not about the fundraiser, anyway.

Not only was the fashion show designed to raise money for LBC, it was also a showcase for LeBlanc's new jewelry line. The buzz for it had grown to a fever pitch, which, in turn, put the spotlight on the charity. Who would have thought that Xavier and Val could combine forces in such a seamless way?

Laurel and Sabrina, that's who. Laurel and Val's wife had become fast friends, burning the midnight oil to help pull this thing together. Xavier couldn't believe how hard the two women had worked, but he showed Laurel how much he appreciated her every night when they finally rolled into bed together.

They did everything together now, including showers and shopping. Xavier had never been happier to have given someone a second chance. He had reaped enormous rewards for it. She felt the same. How did he know? Because her actions always spoke louder than her words. Though she had plenty of those, and she told him often that she loved him, which he wouldn't mind hearing daily for the next fifty years.

Tonight, he hoped to permanently etch that into stone. A diamond, to be precise.

"You have the ring, right?" Val said in his car as they stood at the back of the venue monitoring the show. "I cannot tell you how many favors I had to call in to get that thing done in time."

As Xavier surveyed the crowd, he noted that several celebrities they'd invited had shown. Val had been schmoozing them in order to get signatures on the dotted line for a new LeBlanc advertising campaign and their presence here meant he'd sealed the deal.

In response to Val's question, Xavier patted his pocket, where the one-of-a-kind diamond engagement ring nestled inside a velvet box. "I would have slept with it, but I didn't want to ruin the surprise. Laurel loves surprises, you know."

His brother made a face. "You don't say. That's only the nine thousandth time you've told me."

The thought of proposing choked him up a little, but he didn't temper it. Why should he care if Val knew the subject of marriage tripped him up?

"So I'm a little excited to ask the woman I love to marry me. Sue me."

Saying it out loud didn't alter the swirl inside his gut one bit. *Excited* was the wrong word. Nervous, exhilarated, emotional, sick to his stomach that he'd get it so wrong she'd say no. Any of the above might be more accurate.

Rolling his eyes, Val clapped him on the shoulder. "I would have thought you'd be more excited to hear that I got the preliminary numbers from Roger. Le-Blanc Jewelers is going to hit the billion-dollar mark in revenue for the year by the end of this quarter."

Something bright bloomed in Xavier's chest and he grinned at his brother. "You did it!"

"We did it," Val corrected instantly. "You stacked the dominoes, I knocked them over. We're a team and that's why this fundraiser is going to put you over the figure for your goal, as well. Our inheritances are almost locked up."

Funny how the thought of having succeeded didn't make him as happy as catching sight of Laurel Dixon in the crowd did.

He watched her stop to speak to someone on her way to the dais, where she'd announce to the crowd how they could purchase the models' jewelry with all proceeds benefiting LBC. Edward LeBlanc's will had stated Xavier couldn't write a check to cover the ten-million-dollar fundraising goal, but it had not stipulated whether LeBlanc Jewelers could make a sizable donation—which had been Laurel's idea. Her passion for LBC had spilled over as she'd sold both brothers on the idea.

It was a no-brainer to also let her win over the crowd. It was also the perfect time to drop a surprise proposal on her.

She took the stage, which was his cue to move. But he was frozen, all at once. What if this was a mistake? What if she had no interest in getting married? What if—

"Stop freaking out and go propose," Val muttered from behind him as Laurel's brilliant and beautiful voice rang out through the loudspeaker. "She's going to love that ring you designed. I approved the workmanship personally."

"Yeah, yeah." Somehow Xavier got his body moving and he hit the floorboards of the stage.

Laurel glanced over at him expectantly as she smoothly finished her sentence despite the unplanned interruption. Her silvery-gray eyes caught him sideways, warming him, loving him. His ingrained sense of caution vanished in an instant as he strode across the stage to take her hand.

This was right, no question in his mind.

"Laurel." He cleared his throat as she smiled, totally as caught up as he was, her attention on him instead of the hundreds of people watching them. "Before I met you, I spent a lot of time shutting people out and blaming it on the need to be clearheaded in order to run a company. You taught me that no one can do much of anything by themselves, then helped me figure out that I didn't want to, anyway."

Tears splashed down her face but she didn't interrupt, even when he pulled out the box and flipped the lid, letting her get a glimpse of the ultrarare, smoky gray diamond that matched her eyes.

"This is me, down on one knee, asking you to take my hand and jump." When she arched an eyebrow, he realized he'd forgotten to kneel and hastily corrected that mistake by dropping to the platform with a loud thud. "Both knees, then."

The crowd laughed along with Laurel, who promptly got down on her knees, too. Of course she had. That's what she'd always done—ensured he knew they were a team beyond a shadow of a doubt.

And he had none.

"Yes," she said into the microphone attached to the neckline of her dress. "I'll marry you, but only if you buy me that Jada Ness necklace on the third model as an engagement present. Did you guys see that thing? Gorgeous!"

With that, she turned off her microphone and dove into his arms for a scorching kiss that got the entire crowd cheering and hooting.

"Driving up the price of LeBlanc's donations?" he murmured when they finally came up for air.

She shot him a misty smile. "You see right through me."

How could an inheritance compare with this

woman? It couldn't. And that was the real lesson he suspected his father had intended for his sons to learn.

Nothing could replace the people you let into your life.

* * * * *

Don't miss Xavier's brother Val's story
Wrong Brother, Right Man

To inherit his fortune, flirtatious
Valentino LeBlanc must swap roles with his
too-serious brother. He'll prove he's just as good
as, if not better than, his brother.
At everything. But when he hires
his brother's ex to advise him,
things won't stay professional for long...

Available now!
Only from USA TODAY bestselling
author Kat Cantrell!

#2617 MOST ELIGIBLE TEXAN
Texas Cattleman's Club: Bachelor Auction
by Jules Bennett
Tycoon Matt Galloway's going up on the bachelor auction block, but there's only one woman he wants bidding on him—his best friend's widow. Then his plans to seduce the gorgeous single mom get *really* complicated when old secrets come to light...

#2618 THE BILLIONAIRE'S LEGACY
Billionaires and Babies • by Reese Ryan
When tech billionaire Benjamin Bennett returns home for his cousin's wedding, a passionate weekend with his former crush—his older sister's best friend, Sloane Sutton—results in *two* surprises. But can he get past Sloane's reasons for refusing to marry him for the twins' sakes?

#2619 TEMPT ME IN VEGAS
by Maureen Child
Cooper Hayes should have inherited his partner's half of their Vegas hotel empire. Instead, the man's secret daughter is now part owner! The wide-eyed beauty is ill suited for wheeling and dealing, and Cooper *will* buy her out. But not before he takes her to his bed...

#2620 HOT CHRISTMAS KISSES
Love in Boston • by Joss Wood
International power broker Matt Edwards can never be more than an on-again, off-again hookup to DJ Winston. But when he moves to Boston and becomes part of her real life—carrying secrets with him—their red-hot chemistry explodes. Will they finally face the feelings they've long denied?

#2621 RANCHER UNTAMED
Cole's Hill Bachelors • by Katherine Garbera
When wealthy rancher Diego Velasquez donates one night to the highest bidder, he's bought by a nanny! But after one fiery encounter, beautiful Pippa slips away, driven by secrets she can't reveal. Now this Texan vows he'll learn the truth and have her back in his arms!

#2622 THE BOYFRIEND ARRANGEMENT
Millionaires of Manhattan • by Andrea Laurence
Sebastian said yes to Harper's fake-boyfriend scheme—because he couldn't resist! Now, as her date at a destination wedding, every dance, every touch, every kiss makes him want more. But when a blackmailer reveals everything, will they choose to turn this false romance into something real?

HDCNM0918

*When tech billionaire Benjamin Bennett returns home
for his cousin's wedding, a passionate weekend with his
former crush—his elder sister's best friend
Sloane Sutton—results in two surprises. But can he get
past Sloane's reasons for refusing to marry him
for the twins' sakes?*

Read on for a sneak peek of
The Billionaire's Legacy *by Reese Ryan,
part of the Billionaires and Babies series!*

Benjamin Bennett was a catch by anyone's standards—
even before you factored in his healthy bank account.
But he was her best friend's little brother. And though he
was all grown-up now, he was just a kid compared to her.

Flirting with Benji would start tongues wagging all
over Magnolia Lake. Not that she cared what they thought
of her. But if the whole town started talking, it would
make things uncomfortable for the people she loved.

"Thanks for the dance."

Benji lowered their joined hands but didn't let go.
Instead, he leaned down, his lips brushing her ear and his
well-trimmed beard gently scraping her neck. "Let's get
out of here."

It was a bad idea. A really bad idea.

Her cheeks burned. "But it's your cousin's wedding."

He nodded toward Blake, who was dancing with his

bride, Savannah, as their infant son slept on his shoulder. The man was in complete bliss.

"I doubt he'll notice I'm gone. Besides, you'd be rescuing me. If Jeb Dawson tells me one more time about his latest invention—"

"Okay, okay." Sloane held back a giggle as she glanced around the room. "You need to escape as badly as I do. But there's no way we're leaving here together. It'd be on the front page of the newspaper by morning."

"Valid point." Benji chuckled. "So meet me at the cabin."

"The cabin on the lake?" She had so many great memories of weekends spent there.

It would just be two old friends catching up on each other's lives. Nothing wrong with that.

She repeated it three times in her head. But there was nothing friendly about the sensations that danced along her spine when he'd held her in his arms and pinned her with that piercing gaze.

"Okay. Maybe we can catch up over a cup of coffee or something."

"Or something." The corner of his sensuous mouth curved in a smirk.

A shiver ran through her as she wondered, for the briefest moment, how his lips would taste.

Don't miss
The Billionaire's Legacy *by Reese Ryan,*
part of the Billionaires and Babies series!

Available October 2018 wherever
Harlequin® Desire books and ebooks are sold.

www.Harlequin.com

"What's the worst that could happen?" Wyatt asked.

I could get hurt.

Except Lindy didn't need anything from Wyatt. Nothing but his body, anyway. If, in theory, she were to give in to their attraction. He couldn't take anything from her. Not her house, not her land. And if she didn't love him, he couldn't take her self-respect, he couldn't take her heart, and he couldn't give her any pain.

Really, what was the point of going through the trauma of ending a ten-year marriage if you didn't learn something from it? If she knew this was only going to be physical, only temporary...

What was the worst that could happen?

"I..."

He leaned in, his face a whisper from hers. And oh... The way he smelled. Like sunshine and hay. Hard work and something that was just him. Only him.

She wondered if he would taste just the same.

She was about to find out, she knew. He was leaning in, so close now.

She wanted... She wanted to kiss him.

She wanted to kiss another man, finally. To take that step to move on. But more than that, she wanted to kiss Wyatt Dodge more than she wanted to breathe.

And bless him for taking the control. Something she never thought she would think, ever. But he was going to take the decision away from her, and she wasn't going to have to answer his questions, wasn't going to have to do a single thing other than stand there and be kissed.

She was ready.

He squeezed her chin gently, pressing his thumb down on her lower lip, and then he released his hold on her, taking a step back. "Think on it," he said.

"I… *What?*"

But he was already moving away from her. "Think on it, Lindy," he said, turning around and strolling away from her.

She looked around, incredulous. But the street was empty, and there was no one to shout her outrage to.

And damn that man, she still wanted him to kiss her.

***

Good Time Cowboy
by New York Times *bestselling author Maisey Yates,
available September 2018 wherever
HQN Books and ebooks are sold.*

www.HQNBooks.com

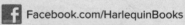
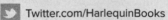
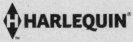